"Whimsical Wonders

50 Tales of Fictional Fun"

Copyright

CONTENTS

Note: These Story Ideas Are Original And Have Not
Been Previously Published.

1

The Dancing Donut

---◦◇◦---

Once upon a time, in a small town, there was a bakery named "Sweet Delights" that was known for its delicious donuts. The bakery was run by a kind old woman named Martha, who had been baking for as long as she could remember.

One day, Martha created a very special donut. It was covered in rainbow sprinkles, and had a secret ingredient that made it irresistible. As soon as the donut was placed in the display case, it began to dance!

The customers were amazed and delighted by the dancing donut, and word of it quickly spread. People from neighboring towns came to see the donut dance, and Sweet Delights became famous for it.

However, not everyone was happy about the dancing donut's success. A rival bakery owner, named Mr. Crumble, became jealous and decided to steal the secret ingredient. He sneaked into Sweet

Delights at night and stole the recipe for the dancing donut.

The next day, Mr. Crumble made his own version of the dancing donut and put it in his display case. However, when he tried to make it dance, it just sat there like an ordinary donut.

Customers were disappointed and Mr. Crumble became the laughing stock of the town. Meanwhile, Martha continued to make the original dancing donut, and her bakery became more popular than ever.

In the end, Mr. Crumble realized that it wasn't just the secret ingredient that made the donut dance - it was the love and care that Martha put into her baking. He apologized for his actions and Martha forgave him.

From then on, the two bakeries worked together to make the town a sweeter and happier place. And the dancing donut continued to delight customers with its magical moves for many years to come.

As time passed, Martha became old and frail, and she knew that she could no longer run the bakery on her own. She decided to pass on the recipe for the dancing donut to her granddaughter, Lily, who had always been fascinated by her grandmother's baking.

Lily was thrilled to inherit the recipe, and she promised to continue the legacy of Sweet Delights. However, she was also nervous - could she ever make a donut as delicious as her grandmother's?

One day, as she was baking, Lily accidentally spilled some of the secret ingredient onto the floor. She tried to clean it up, but it seemed like it had vanished into thin air.

That night, she went to bed feeling worried and upset. However, she was awakened by a strange sound coming from the kitchen. When she went to investigate, she saw something that she could hardly believe - the spilled ingredient had formed itself into a tiny dancing donut!

Lily was amazed and delighted. She knew that this was a sign from her grandmother, and that she could continue the legacy of Sweet Delights with confidence.

From that day forward, Lily continued to make the dancing donut with love and care, just as her grandmother had before her. And the donut continued to dance its way into the hearts of customers old and new, spreading joy and sweetness wherever it went.

2

The Mischievous Mermaid

————•◦◇◦•————

Once upon a time, in a sparkling blue ocean, lived a mischievous mermaid named Pearl. Pcarl was known throughout the ocean for her playful pranks and her love of adventure.

One day, while exploring a nearby shipwreck, Pearl stumbled upon a magical pearl. The pearl granted her the power to transform into a human for one day each year.

Pearl was thrilled with her newfound ability, and couldn't wait to experience life on land. She waited anxiously for the day when she could use her power.

Finally, the day arrived. Pearl transformed into a beautiful human girl and made her way onto land. She was amazed by all the new sights and sounds around her - the bustling streets, the bright colors, and the delicious smells.

However, Pearl's mischievous nature soon got the better of her. She began to play pranks on the humans, such as tickling them or stealing their hats.

At first, the humans found her antics amusing, but soon they became annoyed and even angry.

One day, Pearl played a prank on a group of fishermen, causing them to lose their catch. They were furious, and they set out to capture her.

Pearl realized too late that she had gone too far. She tried to escape, but the humans were too fast for her. They captured her and brought her back to their village, where they put her in a small tank.

Pearl was miserable in the tank, and she longed to return to the ocean. She knew that she had only herself to blame for her predicament.

As she lay in the tank, Pearl heard the sound of a familiar voice. It was a friendly dolphin that she had met on her adventures in the ocean. The dolphin had followed her to land and had come to rescue her.

Together, Pearl and the dolphin made their way back to the ocean. Pearl was grateful for her friend's help, and she realized that she had learned an important lesson - that her pranks could have serious consequences, and that she needed to think before she acted.

From that day forward, Pearl continued to enjoy her adventures in the ocean, but she was much more careful about the pranks she played on humans. And whenever she thought about her misadventures on land, she couldn't help but smile at the memory of her mischievous mermaid days.

As Pearl swam through the ocean, she came across a school of young mermaids who were intrigued by her tales of her adventure on land. Pearl realized that she had the opportunity to teach them about the importance of responsibility and making good choices.

She shared her story with the young mermaids, and they listened with rapt attention. Pearl's tale taught them the value of thinking before acting and considering how their actions could impact others. The young mermaids took Pearl's lesson to heart and promised to always act responsibly and make good choices.

Pearl was thrilled to have made a positive impact on the young mermaids, and she continued to explore the ocean with a newfound sense of purpose. She learned that adventure and fun could coexist with responsibility and that making good choices was the key to living a fulfilling life.

Years passed, and Pearl became known throughout the ocean not just for her playful pranks but for her wisdom and guidance to the younger generations of mermaids. She became a beloved member of the ocean community, and her legacy lived on through the generations of mermaids she had taught and inspired.

And as she looked back on her life, Pearl knew that her mischievous nature had led her to incredible adventures and had taught her valuable lessons. She smiled contentedly, knowing that she had lived a life full of joy, laughter, and meaning.

3

The Adventures of Furry the Feline

—•◦◇◦•—

Once upon a time, in a cozy little house on the edge of town, lived a fluffy, orange cat named Furry. Furry was a curious and adventurous feline, always eager to explore and discover new things.

One day, Furry decided to venture beyond the familiar surroundings of his home and into the vast and mysterious outdoors. As he ventured further into the unknown, he encountered a whole world of new sights, sounds, and smells.

Furry was thrilled by all the new discoveries he made on his adventure. He met a friendly squirrel who taught him how to climb trees, a chatty blue jay who shared stories of his travels, and a wise old owl who gave him advice on how to navigate the dangers of the outdoors.

But Furry's adventure was not without its challenges. He encountered a pack of stray dogs who chased him through the streets, a thunderstorm that left him soaked and shivering, and a cranky old tomcat who warned him to stay away from his territory.

Despite the challenges, Furry was determined to continue his adventure. He learned to use his wits and agility to avoid danger, and he made new friends along the way.

As the days turned into weeks and the weeks turned into months, Furry's adventures became legendary in the neighborhood. People would gather around to hear stories of his daring exploits, and children would delight in his antics.

Eventually, Furry returned to his cozy little house, tired but happy from his adventures. He knew that he had seen and experienced things that most cats could only dream of, and he was content to spend the rest of his days at home, snuggled up in his favorite spot by the window.

But even as he dozed off into a contented slumber, Furry knew that there were still adventures to be had and mysteries to be uncovered. And with a satisfied purr, he dreamed of the new discoveries that awaited him on his next adventure.

And so, Furry continued to explore and discover the world around him. He ventured into new neighborhoods, made new friends, and even helped rescue a kitten who had gotten stuck in a tree.

But one day, Furry's adventures took him farther than he had ever gone before. He found himself in a dense forest, surrounded by towering trees and unfamiliar creatures.

As he explored deeper into the forest, Furry heard a faint meowing coming from a nearby bush. He cautiously approached the bush and found a tiny kitten, shivering and scared.

Furry knew that he had to help the kitten, so he carefully picked her up in his mouth and carried her back to the safety of his home.

From that day on, Furry had a new companion to join him on his adventures. Together, they explored the world around them, discovering new sights and sounds and making new friends along the way.

And as they curled up together at night, exhausted but happy from their adventures, Furry knew that he had found a true friend and companion for life.

4

The Time-Traveling Turtle

———◦◇◦———

Once upon a time, in a quiet pond at the edge of a forest, lived a small green turtle named Timmy. Timmy was not like other turtles - he had a strange fascination with time and was convinced that he could travel through it.

One day, Timmy found an old watch that had been discarded by a nearby hiker. He picked up the watch in his mouth and began to swim around the pond, focusing all his energy on the watch and willing himself to travel through time.

Suddenly, Timmy felt a jolt and found himself transported to a new time period. He looked around in amazement as he saw strange creatures and unfamiliar sights.

Over time, Timmy became an expert at time-traveling, journeying through history and experiencing new adventures in each era. He traveled to ancient Egypt and saw the construction of the great pyramids. He visited the Middle Ages and witnessed knights in shining armor battling fierce dragons. He even traveled to the future and saw the incredible technological advancements of humanity.

Despite his incredible experiences, Timmy never forgot his true home in the quiet pond. He would always return to his pond, telling the other animals about his adventures and showing them the treasures he had collected from his travels.

As Timmy grew older, he began to worry that he would never find a way to stay in his favorite time period forever. But one day, he realized that he didn't need to travel through time to live a fulfilling life. He could experience new adventures and discoveries right in his own pond.

From that day on, Timmy spent his days exploring the pond and discovering new things. He made new friends, found new treasures, and lived a happy and contented life in his own time and place.

And as he looked back on his life, Timmy knew that his time-traveling adventures had taught him an important lesson - that sometimes, the greatest discoveries are waiting right in front of us, if only we have the eyes to see them.

But even as Timmy settled into a comfortable life in his pond, he couldn't resist the urge to travel through time and explore new eras. So, he continued to experiment with different methods of time-traveling.

One day, Timmy discovered an old, mysterious artifact that had washed up on the shores of his pond. It was a glowing crystal that pulsed with a strange energy, and Timmy felt an intense curiosity about it.

He cautiously approached the crystal and concentrated all his energy on it. Suddenly, he felt a powerful surge of energy, and he found himself hurtling through time and space once again.

This time, however, Timmy found himself in a dangerous and unfamiliar era. He was in the midst of a war between two powerful kingdoms, with weapons and destruction all around him.

Despite the danger, Timmy knew that he had to use his time-traveling abilities to make a difference in this world. He used his knowledge of the future to help the weaker kingdom win the war, and he became a legendary hero in that era.

After several years of fighting, Timmy eventually found his way back to his own time and pond. He was older, wiser, and more experienced than ever before. And although he had seen many incredible things in his time-traveling adventures, he knew that there was no place like home.

From that day on, Timmy continued to live a peaceful life in his pond, surrounded by the friends and treasures that he had accumulated over the years. But he never forgot the incredible adventures that he had experienced, and he knew that he would always be a time-traveling turtle at heart.

5

The Curious Case of the Talking Plant

———•◇◦•———

In a small garden in the middle of a bustling city, there was a plant unlike any other. It was a tall, leafy green plant that had an uncanny ability to speak.

The plant's name was Leo, and he was well-known among the animals and insects in the garden. Leo would spend his days chatting with the busy bees, singing songs with the chirping crickets, and trading stories with the fluttering butterflies.

One day, Leo's curious nature got the better of him, and he decided to explore beyond the garden. He wanted to see what the world beyond the garden's walls was like and discover new wonders that he had never seen before.

So, Leo set out on a journey of discovery, traveling through fields, forests, and mountains. Along the way, he met all kinds of creatures and plants, each with their unique stories and personalities.

But as Leo traveled farther from home, he began to notice something strange. Everywhere he went, the plants were dying, and the animals were getting sick. Leo knew that he had to do something to help.

He remembered the stories that the wise old oak tree had told him about the importance of nature and how all living things were connected. Leo realized that the plants and animals were all part of a delicate ecosystem, and he needed to find a way to restore balance to the world.

So, Leo decided to use his unique gift of speech to spread the message of environmental conservation. He spoke to everyone he met, telling them about the dangers of pollution, deforestation, and climate change. He rallied plants and animals alike, urging them to work together to protect the planet that they all called home.

Over time, Leo's message began to spread, and more and more creatures joined his cause. They worked tirelessly to plant new trees, clean up polluted rivers, and create sustainable habitats for all living things.

And so, Leo became known as the hero of the natural world. His curious nature and unique gift of speech had allowed him to make a real difference in the world, and he had shown everyone the power of a determined heart and a passionate voice.

Leo eventually made his way back to the small garden where he had started his journey. But when he arrived, he found that the garden had changed. The once-bustling garden was now a desolate wasteland, with wilted flowers, dry soil, and sickly animals.

Leo realized that he had been gone for too long, and he had neglected his duties as the guardian of the garden. He knew that he had to act quickly to restore the garden to its former glory.

Using the lessons he had learned on his journey, Leo set to work. He enlisted the help of the animals and insects, and together they worked to restore the soil, plant new seeds, and create a sustainable ecosystem.

Months passed, and slowly but surely, the garden began to come back to life. The flowers bloomed once again, the bees buzzed happily, and the animals thrived in their new, healthy environment.

And as Leo looked out over the garden that he had saved, he knew that his journey had been worth it. He had explored the world, met incredible creatures, and learned valuable lessons about the importance of nature and the power of speech.

But most importantly, he had found his true calling as the guardian of the garden. And as he settled back into his role, he knew that he would always be there to protect and nurture the natural world around him.

6

The Secret Life of Socks

—•◇•—

Socks are an essential part of our daily lives. They keep our feet warm and protected, and they come in all shapes, sizes, and colors. But what if there was more to socks than meets the eye?

In "The Secret Life of Socks," we follow the journey of a pair of ordinary socks as they go through their daily routine. But when night falls, the socks come to life, and a whole new world unfolds.

The socks, named Charlie and Lucy, have a secret hideout where they meet with other socks from all over the world. There's Hector, a bright red sock from Spain, and Kimmy, a striped sock from Japan. Together, they form the Sock Society, an underground organization dedicated to helping socks everywhere.

Their mission is to ensure that every sock in the world is treated with respect and dignity. They provide aid to socks that have been lost or separated from their mates, and they fight against sock discrimination.

But their biggest challenge comes when a group of rogue socks, led by the notorious Black Sock, starts to terrorize the sock community. The Black Sock and his gang believe that socks should rule the world and that humans are inferior.

Charlie and Lucy, along with their friends in the Sock Society, must come up with a plan to stop the rogue socks before it's too late. They use their unique sock skills, like stretching and flexibility, to sneak around undetected and gather intelligence on the Black Sock's plans.

Finally, the day of the showdown arrives. The Sock Society and the rogue socks face off in an epic battle, with sock versus sock, in a race to determine the fate of the sock world.

In the end, the Sock Society triumphs, and the rogue socks are banished to the land of lost socks. Charlie and Lucy return to their human owner's drawer, satisfied that they have protected the world of socks and their human friends.

But as they settle into their drawer, they can't help but wonder what other secrets and adventures await them in the world of socks. The Secret Life of Socks is full of surprises, and you never know what you'll find when you take a closer look at your sock drawer.

As the days passed, Charlie and Lucy couldn't shake the feeling that they were meant for something more than just being worn and tossed in the laundry. They wanted to continue their work with the Sock Society and help other socks in need.

One day, they overheard their human owner talking about a sock drive at a local shelter. The shelter was in desperate need of socks for their residents, who were homeless and struggling to stay warm during the cold winter months.

Charlie and Lucy knew that this was their chance to make a difference. They snuck out of the drawer and made their way to the shelter, where they found hundreds of lonely and mismatched socks piled up in a corner.

With their sock skills and the help of the Sock Society, they sorted through the socks and matched them up, creating pairs and making sure that every sock found a mate. They even patched up a few of the socks that had holes or were worn out, using thread from their own fibers.

When they were finished, the pile of socks was transformed into neat rows of matching pairs, ready to be distributed to the shelter residents. The Sock Society was thrilled with the success of the sock drive and grateful to Charlie and Lucy for their hard work.

From that day forward, Charlie and Lucy continued to find ways to help socks in need. They volunteered at the shelter, visited schools to teach children about sock safety and hygiene, and even organized a sock recycling program to reduce waste and protect the environment.

And while they still had their secret meetings and adventures with the Sock Society, they had found a new purpose in life. They knew that their socks were more than just pieces of clothing; they were important members of society, with their own unique skills and abilities.

So the next time you slip on a pair of socks, remember that they may have a secret life and a mission to help others. And if you listen carefully, you might just hear them whispering about their latest adventure in the world of socks.

7

The Enchanted Mirror

Once upon a time in a faraway kingdom, there was an enchanted mirror that had been passed down from generation to generation. This mirror was no ordinary mirror, as it had the power to grant wishes to those who looked into it.

The mirror was guarded by a powerful sorceress named Mirabelle, who lived deep in the forest. Mirabelle was the only one who knew how to use the mirror's power and was tasked with protecting it from those who would use it for evil.

One day, a young princess named Isabella stumbled upon the enchanted mirror while wandering in the forest. She was entranced by its beauty and couldn't resist looking into it. As she gazed into the mirror, she wished for a life of adventure and excitement.

To her surprise, her wish was granted, and she was transported to a magical world filled with dragons, unicorns, and talking animals. Isabella soon discovered that her wish had come with a price, as she found herself in the middle of a dangerous quest to save the kingdom from an evil sorcerer who had been threatening its peace and prosperity.

With the help of a brave knight named Sir Edward, Isabella set out on a perilous journey to defeat the sorcerer and restore order to the kingdom. Along the way, they encountered many challenges and obstacles, but they never lost hope or gave up on their mission.

As they drew closer to the sorcerer's lair, Isabella realized that she had been given the gift of bravery and courage. She was no longer the timid princess who had wished for adventure, but a brave and determined warrior who would do whatever it took to save her kingdom.

In the final battle against the sorcerer, Isabella and Sir Edward fought with all their might, using their newfound skills and the enchanted mirror's power to defeat the sorcerer and restore peace to the kingdom.

As they returned to the castle, Isabella realized that the enchanted mirror had given her more than just adventure and excitement. It had given her the gift of courage, bravery, and the ability to believe in herself.

From that day forward, Isabella dedicated her life to protecting her kingdom and helping others, using the lessons she had learned on her enchanted journey. And the enchanted mirror remained under the watchful eye of Mirabelle, ready to grant wishes to those who looked into it with pure hearts and noble intentions.

But over time, people began to forget about the enchanted mirror and the power it held. It became nothing more than a forgotten relic, collecting dust in Mirabelle's hut in the forest.

Years passed, and the kingdom fell into darkness once again, as a new threat emerged. A wicked sorceress, who had long been banished from the kingdom, returned with an army of dark creatures, intent on destroying everything in her path.

The people of the kingdom were desperate for help, and many turned to the enchanted mirror, hoping to find a way to defeat the sorceress and save their home. But when they looked into the mirror, they saw only their own fears and doubts reflected back at them.

Mirabelle knew that something had to be done to restore the mirror's power and help the people of the kingdom. She set out on a quest to find the source of the mirror's enchantment, traveling to distant lands and seeking out ancient texts and forgotten spells.

After months of searching, Mirabelle finally discovered the source of the mirror's power. She realized that the mirror was not enchanted by magic, but by the hopes and dreams of those who looked into it.

With this newfound knowledge, Mirabelle returned to the kingdom and rallied the people, encouraging them to believe in themselves and their ability to defeat the sorceress. She reminded them that the power of the mirror lay within themselves, and that by working together and believing in their cause, they could overcome any obstacle.

And so, the people of the kingdom joined forces and fought against the sorceress and her army, using the power of their own hopes and dreams to overcome their fears and doubts. In the end, they emerged victorious, and the kingdom was restored to its former glory.

From that day forward, the enchanted mirror was known not just for its power to grant wishes, but for its ability to inspire courage and hope in those who looked into it. And Mirabelle became a legend, known throughout the land as the wise sorceress who had restored the mirror's enchantment and saved the kingdom from darkness.

8

The Flying Fish

In the depths of the ocean, there lived a young fish named Finley. Finley was no ordinary fish, for he had a secret talent - he could fly! He loved nothing more than soaring through the water, leaping and flipping in the air.

But Finley was also different in another way. He didn't quite fit in with the other fish in his school. They laughed at him and teased him for his flying, saying that fish weren't meant to fly and that he should stick to swimming like everyone else.

One day, while soaring above the waves, Finley saw something that would change his life forever - a group of birds flying high above him. He watched in amazement as they swooped and glided through the air, and he realized that he wasn't the only creature who could fly.

Determined to learn more about flying, Finley set out on a journey to find the birds and learn their secrets. He swam for days, dodging dangerous predators and navigating treacherous currents, until he finally reached the surface of the water.

There, he met a wise old seagull named Gilbert, who agreed to teach him how to fly like a bird. Gilbert showed Finley how to use his fins to catch the wind and ride the currents, and soon Finley was soaring through the air like a natural.

But just as Finley was beginning to feel confident in his flying abilities, he heard a cry for help. One of his old fish friends, caught in a fishing net, was struggling to stay alive. Finley knew he had to act fast.

Without hesitation, Finley swooped down and used his flying skills to free his friend from the net. The other fish were amazed at what they saw, and they realized that Finley's flying skills could be useful after all.

From that day forward, Finley became the hero of the school. He used his flying abilities to protect his friends from danger and explore new parts of the ocean. And though the other fish never quite understood his love for flying, they learned to accept him for who he was - the Flying Fish.

Years passed, and Finley continued to soar through the ocean, his flying abilities becoming even more advanced. He explored new parts of the ocean that no fish had ever ventured into before, discovering new species and forming friendships with creatures of all kinds.

But one day, Finley received a message from Gilbert the seagull, who had grown old and tired. Gilbert told Finley that it was time for him to pass on his knowledge to a new generation of birds and fish.

Finley was saddened by Gilbert's news, but he knew that it was time for him to take on the role of teacher. He began to share his flying skills with the younger fish in his school, encouraging them to embrace their differences and never give up on their dreams.

And as he watched his students soar through the water, Finley realized that he had achieved something even greater than flying - he had inspired others to believe in themselves and their abilities, just as Gilbert and the birds had once done for him.

From that day forward, the Flying Fish became not just a hero, but a legend - a symbol of hope and determination for all creatures of the ocean. And though he knew that he could never truly fly like a bird, Finley was content knowing that he had found his own unique way to soar.

9

The Magical Bicycle

---•◇•---

Once upon a time, there was a magical bicycle that had been passed down from generation to generation in a small village. The bicycle was said to have the power to grant wishes to anyone who rode it, but only if they were pure of heart and had a true desire for what they wished.

One day, a young girl named Lily stumbled upon the bicycle while exploring the woods. She was a kind and gentle soul, and her heart was filled with a deep longing to see her sick mother recover from her illness.

Without hesitation, Lily climbed onto the bicycle and pedaled away, focusing all her thoughts on her mother's health. As she rode, the bicycle seemed to glow with a warm, golden light, and a sense of peace and calm washed over Lily.

Suddenly, the bicycle jolted to a stop, and a small, glowing creature appeared before her. It was a fairy, and it spoke to Lily in a gentle voice.

"What is it that you wish for, dear child?" the fairy asked.

"I wish for my mother's health to be restored," Lily replied without hesitation.

The fairy smiled and waved its wand, and a gentle breeze swept over Lily. When she looked up, she saw that she was no longer in the woods but back in her village, standing outside her home.

Lily hurried inside to find her mother sitting up in bed, looking healthier and happier than she had in weeks. Overwhelmed with gratitude, Lily knew that the magical bicycle had granted her wish.

From that day on, Lily visited the bicycle often, always with a pure heart and a true desire to help others. And the magical bicycle continued to grant wishes, bringing hope and happiness to all who rode it.

As news of the magical bicycle spread throughout the village, people from all over came to make their wishes. Some wished for wealth, others for love, and still, others for happiness.

But the bicycle was selective, and only those with pure hearts and noble intentions were granted their wishes. Those who wished for selfish gains were left disappointed.

Years passed, and the magical bicycle remained in the village, a source of hope and wonder for all who knew of it. Lily grew up and became a wise and respected elder in the community, always teaching others the importance of kindness, generosity, and pure intentions.

Eventually, the time came for Lily to pass on the magical bicycle to the next generation. She selected a young boy named Thomas, who had shown himself to be kind, humble, and full of compassion for others.

Thomas rode the bicycle, and as he pedaled, he thought deeply about his wish. Finally, he spoke it aloud: "I wish for the world to be a kinder and more peaceful place."

The fairy appeared before him and smiled. "Your wish is a noble one," she said, waving her wand. "May it be granted."

With that, Thomas felt a warm glow surround him, and a sense of peace and hope filled his heart. He knew that his wish had been granted, and that he had been chosen to continue the legacy of the magical bicycle.

And so, the magical bicycle continued to be a source of wonder and hope for generations to come, always granting wishes to those with pure hearts and noble intentions, and spreading kindness, generosity, and compassion throughout the world.

10

The Case of the Missing Moon

——•◦◇◦•——

One night, as the villagers of a small town looked up at the sky, they noticed that something was different. The moon, which usually shone brightly, was nowhere to be seen. It was as if it had vanished into thin air.

The villagers were perplexed and worried. They relied on the moon to guide their way in the dark and mark the passage of time. They knew that something had to be done to find out what had happened to it.

They decided to call on the help of a famous detective, Sherlock Holmes. Sherlock arrived in the town and immediately set to work investigating the case of the missing moon.

He started by talking to the villagers, trying to gather information about the last time they had seen the moon. Most of them remembered seeing it the previous night, but no one had noticed anything out of the ordinary.

Sherlock then looked up at the sky himself, examining the stars and the other celestial bodies. He noticed that the stars were particularly bright, which seemed unusual to him.

He then decided to explore the surrounding area, searching for any clues that might lead him to the missing moon. As he walked through the woods, he stumbled upon a small, hidden cave.

Inside the cave, he found something astonishing. The moon was there, suspended in mid-air by a series of intricate ropes and pulleys. It had been carefully hidden away, as if someone had intentionally taken it from the sky.

Sherlock quickly deduced that this was the work of a group of thieves, who had devised a clever plan to steal the moon and sell it on the black market. He carefully examined the ropes and pulleys, taking note of any clues that might lead him to the culprits.

He then set out to gather evidence and interview suspects, eventually piecing together the whole story. With his clever mind and sharp wit, he was able to track down the thieves and retrieve the moon, returning it to the sky where it belonged.

The villagers were overjoyed to see the moon once again, and they thanked Sherlock for his heroic efforts. The case of the missing moon had been solved, and the town could once again rely on the celestial body to guide them in the darkness of the night.

As a reward for his outstanding detective work, the grateful villagers threw a big feast in Sherlock's honor. They toasted to his success and sang songs of praise for his brilliance and cunning.

Sherlock was pleased with the outcome of the case but remained humble, knowing that it was his duty to use his intelligence for the greater good. He shared his wisdom and knowledge with the villagers, teaching them how to be more observant and analytical in their daily lives.

The villagers listened intently, eager to learn from the master detective. They realized that they too could use their own powers of observation and deduction to solve problems and mysteries that might arise in their community.

The case of the missing moon had brought the town together, strengthening their sense of community and reminding them of the importance of working together towards a common goal. They knew that they could rely on one another in times of trouble, and that their collective intelligence and resourcefulness would always prevail.

Years later, as Sherlock looked up at the sky, he couldn't help but smile, remembering the case of the missing moon. He knew that his work had made a lasting impact on the town, and that his legacy would continue to inspire future generations to use their minds and hearts for the greater good.

11

The Brave Little Ladybug

Once upon a time, in a lush green garden, there lived a brave little ladybug named Lila. Lila was a curious and adventurous bug, always eager to explore the vast and beautiful garden.

One day, as Lila was flying around the garden, she came across a group of ants who were in distress. Their colony was being threatened by a group of greedy grasshoppers, who wanted to take all their food and leave them with nothing.

Lila knew she had to do something to help. She flew over to the ants and asked what was wrong. The ants explained the situation to her, and Lila knew she had to act fast.

Without hesitation, Lila flew over to the grasshoppers' den, determined to confront them and put an end to their thievery. When she arrived, the grasshoppers laughed at her, telling her that she was too small and weak to stop them.

But Lila was not deterred. She flew straight into the grasshoppers' leader, the biggest and meanest of them all. The grasshopper swatted at her, but Lila was quick and nimble, dodging his attacks with ease.

She then flew straight into his eyes, blinding him temporarily. While he was disoriented, Lila grabbed a nearby twig and used it to knock him over. The other grasshoppers were so shocked by her bravery that they fled, never to be seen again.

The ants were overjoyed by Lila's bravery and thanked her profusely. From that day forward, they referred to her as the bravest bug in the garden, and Lila became a hero to all the insects.

Word of Lila's heroism soon spread throughout the garden, and animals of all kinds came to pay their respects to the brave little ladybug. Lila was proud of herself, but she remained humble, knowing that she had only done what she felt was right.

Years later, as Lila flew around the garden, she remembered the day she had stood up to the grasshoppers and protected the ants. She smiled, knowing that her bravery had made a difference in the world, and that she had inspired others to be brave and stand up for what was right.

From that day forward, Lila became a beloved figure in the garden, known for her courage and her unwavering dedication to justice. She continued to explore the garden, always on the lookout for anyone in need of her help.

Over time, Lila became something of a legend in the garden. Many of the younger bugs looked up to her, eager to follow in her footsteps and become heroes themselves.

One day, a young grasshopper approached Lila, asking for her help in stopping a group of wasps who were terrorizing his family. Lila could have easily turned him away, given the way that the grasshoppers had treated her in the past. But instead, she listened to his plight and promised to do everything in her power to help.

Together, Lila and the young grasshopper hatched a plan to stop the wasps. They recruited the help of a group of bees, who were eager to repay Lila for her help in the past. With their combined efforts, they were able to drive off the wasps and restore peace to the grasshoppers' family.

As she flew back to her home in the garden, Lila felt a deep sense of satisfaction. She had helped to bring peace to the garden once again, and she had shown that even the most unlikely of allies could work together to accomplish great things.

Over the years, Lila continued to be a beacon of hope and inspiration to all who knew her. And though she was just a little ladybug, her bravery and kindness had made a big impact on the world around her.

12

The Story of the Singing Spider

—◦◇◦—

Once upon a time, in a forest filled with tall trees and buzzing insects, there lived a small and curious spider named Arachne. She was different from the other spiders in the forest, as she had a beautiful singing voice that she loved to use.

Every day, Arachne would spin her web in the treetops and sing songs of joy and happiness. Her melodies were so enchanting that they would draw in all the animals in the forest, who would stop to listen and enjoy her music.

One day, a group of humans stumbled upon the forest, and they were amazed to hear the sound of singing coming from the treetops. They searched the forest for the source of the music until they found Arachne, perched atop her web, singing her heart out.

The humans were captivated by Arachne's beautiful voice and decided to capture her so that they could take her back to their village and make her sing for them all the time. But when they tried to grab her, Arachne used her quick reflexes to escape their grasp and retreat to the safety of the treetops.

Undeterred, the humans returned to the forest every day, hoping to capture Arachne and take her away with them. But each time they tried, Arachne would use her singing voice to charm and distract them, allowing her to escape once again.

Eventually, the humans grew tired of chasing after Arachne and gave up on their quest to capture her. Instead, they began to appreciate her music and would often stop by the forest just to listen to her sing.

Arachne was grateful for the humans' change of heart, and she continued to sing from her web in the treetops, sharing her beautiful voice with all the animals in the forest and anyone who cared to listen.

Years later, as Arachne looked out over the forest, she knew that her music had brought joy and happiness to many. And though she was just a small spider, she had made a big impact on the world around her with her beautiful voice and her indomitable spirit.

Arachne's reputation as the singing spider spread far beyond the forest. People from distant lands would travel to hear her sing, and they would often leave gifts for her in appreciation of her music.

Arachne would use these gifts to improve her web, making it stronger and more intricate with each passing day. And as she spun, she would continue to sing, inspiring those who heard her to find joy in even the darkest of times.

But despite her fame, Arachne never lost her humility or her love for the forest. She remained a creature of the treetops, always looking out over the canopy and singing her songs of joy and happiness.

One day, as Arachne was singing in her web, she heard a familiar voice calling out to her from below. It was a young spider, much like herself, who had heard of Arachne's singing and had come to learn from her.

Arachne welcomed the young spider with open arms and began to teach her the ways of music and web-spinning. Together, they sang and spun, creating a beautiful web filled with harmonies and melodies.

And as Arachne looked at the young spider, she realized that she had become the teacher, passing down the knowledge and love of music that had been given to her so many years ago.

Years passed, and Arachne grew old and frail, but she never lost her love for music or her dedication to the forest. Even as she neared the end of her life, she continued to sing and spin, leaving behind a legacy of beauty and joy that would never be forgotten.

And though she was gone, the memory of Arachne and her singing lived on in the hearts and minds of all those who had been touched by her music. For she had shown that even the smallest and most unlikely creatures can create something beautiful and powerful when they follow their hearts and share their gifts with the world.

13

The Ghostly Gargoyle

—•◇•—

Once upon a time, in a dark and eerie castle, there lived a gargoyle named Grimsley. He was a fearsome creature with a stern expression, and his job was to guard the castle and scare away any unwanted visitors.

But Grimsley had a secret. Despite his fearsome appearance, he was actually quite kind-hearted and loved nothing more than to watch the sunset over the castle walls.

One night, as Grimsley was watching the sunset, he heard a strange noise coming from one of the castle's towers. He cautiously approached the tower, ready to defend the castle against any intruders.

But when he reached the tower, he found no one there. Confused, he searched the tower from top to bottom, but he found nothing. The noise had stopped, and there was no sign of anyone or anything that could have made it.

Grimsley was puzzled by the strange occurrence, but he brushed it off as a figment of his imagination and returned to his post.

But over the next few nights, the strange noises continued, always coming from the same tower. Grimsley became more and more curious about what could be causing the noise, and he decided to investigate further.

Late one night, when the castle was shrouded in darkness, Grimsley made his way up the stairs to the tower. The closer he got, the louder the noise became, until he finally reached the top of the tower and discovered the source of the noise.

It was a ghostly figure, floating in the air and emitting a haunting melody. Grimsley was startled but fascinated by the ghostly apparition, and he listened to the melody with rapt attention.

The ghostly figure noticed Grimsley and approached him, beckoning him to follow. Grimsley hesitated at first, but then he decided to follow the ghostly figure to see where it would lead him.

They floated through the castle, passing through walls and floors until they reached a hidden chamber. In the center of the chamber was a beautiful harp, and the ghostly figure motioned for Grimsley to play it.

Grimsley was hesitant at first, as he had never played a musical instrument before. But then he remembered the haunting melody that the ghostly figure had played and decided to give it a try.

To his surprise, the harp seemed to play itself, and Grimsley was filled with a sense of wonder and joy as he listened to the beautiful music it created. The ghostly figure continued to float nearby, swaying to the music and smiling at Grimsley.

For many nights after that, Grimsley would sneak away to the hidden chamber and play the harp, creating beautiful melodies that echoed through the castle. And though he never saw the ghostly figure again, he knew that he had made a friend and found a new love for music that would stay with him forever.

Over time, Grimsley's music began to have a transformative effect on the castle. The once-dark and dreary halls were filled with light and warmth, and the inhabitants of the castle began to smile and laugh more often.

Even the plants in the castle gardens seemed to flourish and grow more vibrantly under the influence of Grimsley's music. It was as though the music had the power to bring life and joy to all those who heard it.

Eventually, word of Grimsley's music spread beyond the castle walls, and people came from far and wide to hear him play. They were amazed by the beauty of his melodies and the transformative effect that they had on the castle and its inhabitants.

Grimsley became known as the ghostly gargoyle who could make music that could heal the soul. He would play his harp for anyone who would listen, bringing joy and happiness to all who heard him.

And though he remained a fearsome-looking creature, Grimsley was loved and respected by all who knew him. He had discovered a gift that had been hidden within him all along, and he used it to bring light and happiness to the world.

Years went by, and Grimsley grew old and frail, but he never stopped playing his harp. And even after he passed away, his music continued to echo through the castle, bringing joy and peace to all those who heard it.

And so the legend of the ghostly gargoyle lived on, a testament to the power of music to transform even the darkest of places into something beautiful and magical.

14

The Incredible Shrinking Scientist

———•◦◇◦•———

Dr. Benjamin Bloom was a brilliant scientist who was always pushing the boundaries of science. He had dedicated his life to the study of nanotechnology, and he had made several groundbreaking discoveries that had earned him international acclaim.

One day, while working in his lab, Dr. Bloom stumbled upon a new breakthrough. He had discovered a way to shrink matter down to the size of a tiny particle, and he was thrilled with the possibilities that this new technology could bring.

Without thinking, Dr. Bloom decided to try the technology on himself. He shrunk himself down to the size of a pea and stepped out of his lab, eager to explore his surroundings from a whole new perspective.

At first, everything seemed normal. But as Dr. Bloom explored his lab, he began to notice that everything was much larger than he remembered.

The lab equipment towered over him, and even the smallest of sounds seemed to echo around him like thunder.

Dr. Bloom was amazed at the new world he had discovered, but he quickly realized that he was in danger. A single misstep could result in him being crushed or injured, and he had to be careful with every movement he made.

As time passed, Dr. Bloom began to worry that he might be stuck at his tiny size forever. He had no idea how to reverse the effects of his shrinking technology, and he knew that he couldn't continue living his life as a miniature scientist.

Desperate for a solution, Dr. Bloom returned to his lab and began working feverishly to find a way to reverse the effects of his shrinking technology. He worked day and night, experimenting with different compounds and formulas until he finally stumbled upon the solution.

With a sense of relief, Dr. Bloom injected himself with the antidote, and within moments, he began to grow back to his normal size. He stood there, amazed and grateful that he had finally found a way to reverse the effects of his shrinking technology.

From that day on, Dr. Bloom continued his work in nanotechnology, but he did so with a newfound respect for the dangers of pushing the boundaries of science too far. He knew that he had been lucky to survive his experiment, and he made a vow to always be cautious in his pursuit of knowledge and discovery.

Word of Dr. Bloom's incredible shrinking experiment spread quickly throughout the scientific community. Many were intrigued by the potential applications of such technology, but others were cautious and concerned about the risks involved.

Despite the mixed reactions, Dr. Bloom became somewhat of a celebrity within the scientific community. He was invited to speak at conferences and was interviewed by numerous media outlets, all eager to hear about his groundbreaking discovery.

Dr. Bloom was grateful for the attention, but he remained focused on his work. He continued to study nanotechnology and pushed the boundaries of what was possible, but he did so with a newfound sense of caution.

Over time, Dr. Bloom's work led to even more incredible discoveries in the field of nanotechnology. His research led to the development of new materials and technologies that would revolutionize industries ranging from medicine to electronics.

But even as his work continued to make a significant impact on the world, Dr. Bloom never forgot the lessons he had learned from his incredible shrinking experiment. He remained humble and cautious, always mindful of the potential dangers of his work.

And though he continued to make new discoveries and push the boundaries of science, Dr. Bloom never forgot that sometimes the most incredible discoveries can come from the simplest of experiments.

15

The Rainbow Unicorn

Once upon a time, in a magical forest, there lived a beautiful unicorn named Rosalind. Rosalind was not just any ordinary unicorn, she was a rainbow unicorn, with a mane and tail that shone in every color of the rainbow.

The other creatures in the forest marveled at Rosalind's beauty, and she was often sought after to attend parties and other events. But despite her popularity, Rosalind was lonely. She longed for someone to share her adventures with someone who understood her and appreciated her for who she was.

One day, as Rosalind was wandering through the forest, she stumbled upon a small pond. As she looked into the clear water, she saw her reflection staring back at her. But to her surprise, she also saw a second reflection - that of another unicorn, with a mane and tail that shone in the same colors as her own.

Rosalind couldn't believe her eyes. She had never seen another rainbow unicorn before. She approached the water's edge cautiously, and as she did, the other unicorn stepped out from the trees.

The other unicorn introduced herself as Aurora and explained that she had been living in a hidden part of the forest, away from the other creatures. Like Rosalind, Aurora had been longing for someone to share her adventures with.

Over the next few days, Rosalind and Aurora explored the forest together, sharing their stories and discovering new things about each other. They quickly became the best of friends, and they spent all their time together, playing and frolicking through the meadows.

As they explored the forest together, Rosalind and Aurora noticed that there was something special about the way they interacted with the world. The flowers seemed to bloom brighter, and the leaves on the trees shimmered in the sunlight. It was as if their combined joy and happiness was spreading throughout the forest, making everything more beautiful.

And so, Rosalind and Aurora continued to explore the forest, bringing joy and beauty wherever they went. They knew that they were lucky to have found each other, and they vowed to never let anything come between them. For they knew that the world was a better place when they were together.

As Rosalind and Aurora explored the forest, they met many other creatures who were also enchanted by their beauty and friendship. They became known throughout the forest as the Rainbow Unicorns, and soon they were joined by other unicorns with manes and tails of different colors.

Together, they formed a community of unicorns who lived in harmony with the other creatures of the forest. They shared their love and happiness with everyone they met, and the forest became a more joyful place as a result.

But despite their happiness, Rosalind and Aurora knew that there were still challenges ahead. The forest was a magical place, but it was also full of danger. There were wicked creatures that roamed the forest, seeking to harm those who were weaker than themselves.

One day, as Rosalind and Aurora were exploring a dark part of the forest, they were ambushed by a group of trolls. The trolls had heard of the Rainbow Unicorns and were jealous of their beauty and joy. They wanted to capture them and keep them prisoner so that they could never share their joy with the rest of the forest.

Rosalind and Aurora were frightened, but they knew that they had to be brave. They used their magical powers to create a rainbow shield around themselves, and the trolls were unable to penetrate it. They used their hooves to create thunderclaps and their breath to create lightning bolts, and the trolls were driven away.

From that day forward, the Rainbow Unicorns were even more celebrated in the forest. They had proven their bravery and their commitment to each other, and they had shown that their love and joy were stronger than any force of evil.

And so, the Rainbow Unicorns continued to explore the forest, bringing joy and happiness wherever they went. They knew that there would be challenges ahead, but they also knew that as long as they had each other, they could overcome anything that came their way.

16

The Amazing Antics of Anselmo the Aardvark

———•○◇○•———

Anselmo was a curious aardvark who lived in the heart of the African savannah. He spent his days digging through the soil with his long, pointed snout in search of tasty termites and other insects.

But Anselmo was different from the other aardvarks in his community. While they were content to spend their days in the same old tunnels, Anselmo was always looking for new adventures and experiences.

One day, Anselmo discovered a small village on the edge of the savannah. He had never seen humans before, and he was fascinated by their strange customs and habits. He watched as they built houses and tended to their fields, and he was amazed by their ingenuity.

As Anselmo watched the humans, he began to wonder if there was more to life than just digging for insects. He longed to explore the world beyond his tunnels and experience everything that life had to offer.

So, one night, Anselmo snuck out of his burrow and set off on an adventure. He wandered through the savannah, encountering all kinds of creatures, from lions to hyenas to gazelles.

Along the way, Anselmo discovered that he had a talent for singing. He would sit atop termite mounds and sing songs in his deep, rumbling voice, entertaining the other animals who came to listen.

Word of Anselmo's singing talent soon spread throughout the savannah, and he was invited to perform at a festival in a nearby village. Anselmo was nervous at first, but he took a deep breath and belted out a beautiful song that brought tears to the eyes of the humans and animals alike.

After that, Anselmo became something of a celebrity in the savannah. He would travel from village to village, performing his songs and sharing his infectious spirit of adventure.

But even as Anselmo's fame grew, he never forgot his roots as a humble aardvark. He continued to dig for insects and live in his burrow, but he also continued to seek out new adventures and experiences.

And so, Anselmo the aardvark lived a life filled with wonder and amazement, inspiring those around him to live their lives to the fullest and embrace the unknown.

One day, Anselmo heard rumors of a mysterious mountain range far beyond the savannah, and he knew he had to see it for himself. He set off on a long journey, traveling through deserts, jungles, and forests, never losing his sense of wonder and adventure.

Finally, after many weeks of travel, Anselmo reached the mountains. They were even more magnificent than he had imagined, towering high above the clouds and covered in snow and ice.

Anselmo felt a thrill of excitement as he began to climb the mountains, using his sharp claws to scale the steep cliffs. He encountered many challenges along the way, from treacherous crevasses to fierce blizzards, but he never lost his sense of determination and courage.

As he climbed higher and higher, Anselmo felt a sense of awe and wonder at the beauty of the world around him. He had always known that there was more to life than just digging for insects, but now he realized just how vast and wondrous the world truly was.

Finally, after many days of climbing, Anselmo reached the summit of the tallest mountain in the range. He stood at the peak, gazing out at the breathtaking vista of the world below. He felt a sense of peace and contentment, knowing that he had lived his life to the fullest and experienced all the wonders that the world had to offer.

Anselmo descended the mountain, his heart filled with joy and his mind overflowing with memories of his incredible adventure. He returned to his burrow, where he continued to dig for insects and sing his songs, but now he knew that he had seen and experienced more than any other aardvark in the savannah.

And so, Anselmo continued to live a life of adventure and wonder, inspiring others with his courage, determination, and love of life.

17

The Mysterious Message in a Bottle

———•◇•———

One day, a young girl named Lily was walking along the beach when she spotted something bobbing in the waves. As she got closer, she realized it was a bottle, and it had a message inside.

Excited, Lily picked up the bottle and pulled out the message. It was written in a language she couldn't understand, but she could tell it was old, the paper yellowed and crinkled.

Lily was intrigued. She had always loved mysteries, and she sensed that this message was the beginning of an adventure. She took the bottle and the message to her grandfather, who was a retired sailor and had traveled all over the world.

Her grandfather studied the message for a few moments, his brow furrowed in concentration. Finally, he spoke. "This message is written in an ancient language called Phoenician," he said. "It's a language that hasn't been spoken for thousands of years."

Lily was fascinated. "What does it say?" she asked eagerly.

Her grandfather translated the message for her. "It's a message from a sailor who was lost at sea. He writes that he is running out of food and water, and he fears that he will never see his family again. He has no idea where he is, and he is asking for help."

Lily's heart went out to the lost sailor. She knew that she had to find out more. She and her grandfather did some research and discovered that the message was over 2,500 years old. They learned that the sailor had been a member of a Phoenician trading vessel that had sailed from the eastern Mediterranean.

Lily and her grandfather decided to mount an expedition to find out more about the sailor and his fate. They chartered a boat and sailed to the Mediterranean, where they spent weeks exploring ancient ports and studying ancient maps.

Finally, they discovered an ancient record of the Phoenician trading routes, and they were able to determine where the sailor had been when he wrote the message. They found the location on a modern map, and they set sail for the spot where the sailor had been lost.

It was a treacherous journey, but Lily and her grandfather were determined. Finally, they reached the spot where the sailor had written his message. They searched the area for days, but they found nothing.

Just when they were about to give up, they spotted something in the water. It was a wooden chest, and inside was a small, leather-bound journal. Lily and her grandfather opened the journal, and inside, they found the final entry from the lost sailor.

He had written that he had given up hope of ever being rescued, and he was resigned to his fate. But he wrote that he was grateful for the chance to see the world and to experience its wonders, and he hoped that his message would inspire others to do the same.

Lily and her grandfather returned home with the message in a bottle, the sailor's journal, and a newfound appreciation for the wonders of the world and the adventures that lay ahead.

Lily and her grandfather decided to donate the message and the journal to a museum, so that others could learn about the lost sailor's journey and be inspired by his spirit of adventure.

But the experience had sparked something in Lily, and she knew that she wanted to continue exploring the world and uncovering its mysteries. She began studying ancient languages and cultures, and she embarked on her own adventures to discover lost treasures and ancient ruins.

Years later, Lily had become a renowned archaeologist, known for her groundbreaking discoveries and her daring expeditions. But she never forgot the lost sailor who had sparked her passion for adventure, and she always remembered the lesson that he had taught her - to live life to the fullest and to embrace the wonders of the world.

18

The Day the Sun Stopped Shining

———•◦◇◦•———

It was a day like any other, with bright sunshine and clear blue skies. But as the hours passed, people started to notice that something was different. The sun seemed to be getting dimmer and dimmer, until it was just a pale, white disc in the sky.

As the day wore on, the sky grew darker and darker, until it was as black as night. The air grew cold, and people huddled together for warmth and comfort. They could hear strange noises coming from the sky, like thunder and lightning, but without the flashes of light.

As the darkness deepened, people grew afraid. They huddled in their homes, praying for the sun to return. But it didn't. The darkness lasted for days, and people started to panic. Crops withered in the fields, and animals died in the sudden cold.

Scientists worked feverishly to find a solution, but they couldn't figure out what was causing the darkness. Some believed it was a natural phenomenon, like a massive solar storm. Others thought it might be a man-made disaster, caused by pollution or a nuclear accident.

Finally, after a week of darkness, the sun started to return. It was a slow process, with the first light appearing as a faint glow on the horizon. But as the hours passed, the light grew stronger and brighter, until it was once again a warm, golden orb in the sky.

People emerged from their homes, blinking in the sunlight. They looked around at the devastation that had been wrought by the darkness, and they knew that life would never be the same.

Scientists studied the phenomenon for years, trying to understand what had caused the sun to stop shining. Some theories pointed to massive solar flares or magnetic storms, while others blamed human activity and pollution.

But for most people, the day the sun stopped shining was a reminder of how fragile life on Earth truly is, and how important it is to take care of our planet and each other. They vowed to work together to create a better world, one where the sun would always shine bright and warm.

In the years that followed, the world came together to heal and recover from the devastation caused by the darkness. Communities worked to rebuild their homes and farms, and scientists developed new technologies to better understand the sun and its behavior.

But the memory of the dark days lingered, and people never forgot the lessons they had learned. They became more conscious of their impact on the environment and worked harder to reduce pollution and protect the planet.

The event also sparked a renewed interest in space exploration and research. Governments and private companies alike invested in new technologies to study the sun and the universe, hoping to gain a better understanding of the mysteries of the cosmos.

And in the end, the day the sun stopped shining became a turning point for humanity. It served as a reminder of our shared vulnerability, and of the power of science and cooperation to overcome even the most daunting challenges.

19

The Adventures of Ziggy the Zebra

———•◦◇◦•———

Ziggy the Zebra was a curious and adventurous creature, with a love for exploration and discovery. He lived in the African savannah, where he spent his days wandering through the grasslands and interacting with the other animals.

One day, while out for a stroll, Ziggy stumbled upon a hidden trail that he had never seen before. Intrigued, he followed the trail deep into the heart of the savannah, eager to see where it would lead.

As he walked, Ziggy encountered all kinds of animals - lions, elephants, giraffes, and more. They were all surprised to see a zebra wandering so far from home, but Ziggy greeted them with a friendly smile and a wave of his striped tail.

Finally, after hours of walking, Ziggy reached the end of the trail. He found himself at the base of a towering mountain, with a steep, winding path leading up to its summit.

Without hesitation, Ziggy began to climb. It was a difficult journey, with steep inclines and rocky terrain, but Ziggy was determined to reach the top.

At last, he reached the summit, where he was greeted by a stunning view of the savannah stretching out before him. He had never seen anything like it before, and he felt a rush of excitement and awe.

As he gazed out at the breathtaking landscape, Ziggy realized that his adventure had taught him something important - that there was always something new and exciting to discover in the world, and that he should never be afraid to explore and take risks.

From that day forward, Ziggy continued to roam the savannah, always on the lookout for new trails to explore and new adventures to undertake. And he became known as one of the savannah's most fearless and adventurous creatures, inspiring others to follow in his hoofsteps and explore the world around them.

One day, Ziggy heard about a nearby river that was said to be home to a legendary waterfall. The waterfall was said to be the tallest in all of Africa, and many animals had tried and failed to reach it.

But Ziggy was determined to be the first zebra to see the waterfall for himself. He gathered a group of his closest animal friends and set off on the long journey to the river.

The journey was long and challenging, with rocky terrain and treacherous river crossings. But Ziggy and his friends persevered, pushing themselves to their limits and encouraging each other along the way.

Finally, they reached the river and set off downstream. The current was strong, and the water was choppy, but Ziggy led the way with confidence and determination.

After hours of paddling, they heard a distant rumble that grew louder and louder with each passing moment. And then, they saw it - the waterfall.

It was even more magnificent than they had imagined, with water cascading down a sheer cliff face and mist rising up all around them. Ziggy and his friends were awestruck, taking in the sight and sound of the waterfall with wonder and amazement.

As they turned to head back home, Ziggy felt a deep sense of satisfaction and contentment. He knew that he had pushed himself to his limits and achieved something truly remarkable. And he also knew that there were many more adventures and discoveries waiting for him in the wide, wild world.

20

The Misadventures of a Lost Balloon

◦○◇○◦

Once upon a time, there was a happy red balloon named Rosie. She was full of air and soaring high above the city, carried by the wind, and enjoying the view of the bustling streets below.

But Rosie's joy was short-lived when a gust of wind suddenly blew her off course and away from the city. She struggled to stay afloat, but the wind was too strong and she soon found herself tumbling through the air, completely lost.

As Rosie drifted further and further away from the city, she began to feel scared and alone. She wondered if she would ever find her way back home or if she would be lost forever.

Days turned into weeks, and Rosie continued to float aimlessly through the sky, passing over mountains, oceans, and deserts. She encountered all sorts of weather - from fierce storms to scorching heat - and her once-bright red color began to fade and dull from the harsh elements.

Just when Rosie had given up hope of ever finding her way home, she caught a glimpse of something familiar in the distance. It was the city she had been torn away from all those weeks ago.

With a renewed sense of hope and energy, Rosie picked up speed and soared towards the city. She floated over the buildings and parks until she finally spotted a young girl holding a bouquet of balloons.

Rosie knew she had to make her move quickly, so she wiggled and jostled herself free of the other balloons and drifted towards the girl. The girl noticed the red balloon floating towards her and, with a big smile, she reached out and grabbed Rosie's string.

Rosie was filled with joy and relief as she floated alongside the girl, who carried her back to her home in the city. Rosie had finally found her way back home after a long and difficult journey, and she knew that she would never take the feeling of being safe and secure for granted again.

From that day on, Rosie was never alone again. The girl who rescued her became her new best friend, and they went on all sorts of adventures together.

They visited the park, where Rosie got to see all sorts of animals and plants she had never seen before. They even flew through the park's playground, where Rosie was able to see kids playing and having fun.

They also visited the city's museums and art galleries, where Rosie was able to see all sorts of incredible works of art and learn about history and science. She even got to fly through the exhibits, exploring them in a way that no human could.

As time went on, Rosie grew to love her new life with her friend in the city. She knew that she would never forget her misadventures as a lost balloon, but she was also grateful for the new experiences and friendships she had gained.

And whenever Rosie saw another balloon drifting off course, she made sure to reach out and help them find their way back home too. She knew that no balloon should have to face the world alone, and she was determined to be there for anyone who needed her help.

21

Haunted House on Hillside Drive

On a dark and stormy night, a group of friends decided to explore the abandoned house on Hillside Drive. It was rumored to be haunted, but the friends didn't believe in ghosts and were excited to see what they could find.

As they approached the house, they could see that it was in a state of disrepair. The windows were boarded up and the roof was caving in. The door was locked, but one of the friends was able to pick the lock and they all entered the house.

As they walked through the house, they began to feel a strange presence around them. They heard creaks and moans from the old wooden floors and walls, and it felt as if something was watching them from the shadows.

Suddenly, a door slammed shut behind them and they were all trapped. They tried to open the door, but it wouldn't budge. It was as if someone, or something, was holding it shut.

As they continued to explore the house, they found a hidden room with a strange book lying on a table. The book was written in a language they couldn't understand, but they could feel its power emanating from its pages.

The friends began to feel more and more uneasy as they read through the book, and they realized that they had made a grave mistake by coming to the haunted house. They had unknowingly unleashed an evil force that was now trapped inside with them.

They tried to escape, but every door and window was now locked shut. The storm outside raged on, and it was clear that they were not going to be able to leave the house alive.

As the night wore on, the friends began to feel the presence of the evil force getting stronger and stronger. They heard whispers and moans coming from the shadows, and they knew that they were not alone in the house.

In a moment of desperation, they decided to burn the book, hoping that it would destroy the evil force and release them from the house. They set the book on fire and watched as the flames consumed it.

As the book burned, the doors and windows suddenly burst open and the friends were able to escape the haunted house on Hillside Drive. They never spoke of the incident again, but they knew that they had narrowly escaped a terrifying fate. They also knew that they would never underestimate the power of the supernatural again.

After their narrow escape from the haunted house, the friends went their separate ways. But they were all forever changed by the experience.

Some of them became fascinated with the paranormal and dedicated themselves to studying and investigating ghostly phenomena. Others were haunted by nightmares for weeks, unable to shake the feeling of the evil force they had encountered.

But despite their different paths, they all shared a bond that could never be broken. They had faced something truly terrifying together, and that experience had forged a connection between them that would last a lifetime.

Years later, the group decided to reunite and revisit the haunted house on Hillside Drive. They wanted to see if it was still standing, and if the evil force they had encountered was still trapped inside.

When they arrived at the house, they were surprised to find that it had been restored and was now a beautiful bed and breakfast. The new owners had no knowledge of the house's haunted past, and the friends decided not to tell them about their terrifying experience.

But as they walked through the house, they could still feel the presence of the evil force they had encountered years ago. It was as if the house was still haunted, even though it had been transformed into a beautiful retreat.

The friends left the haunted house on Hillside Drive once again, knowing that they had faced something truly terrifying and that they had come out stronger because of it. They knew that the memory of their experience would stay with them forever, and that they would always be connected by the bond they had forged that night.

22

The Secret Island of the Dancing Trees

———•◦◇◦•———

Deep in the heart of the Pacific Ocean lies a mysterious island that is only known to a select few. It is a place of wonder and beauty, where the trees dance and the animals speak.

Legend has it that the island was created by a powerful sorcerer who was looking for a place to hide his secrets. He cast a spell on the island, making it invisible to all but those who knew the secret password.

One day, a group of adventurers stumbled upon the island while sailing through the Pacific. They had heard rumors of a secret island that was said to be inhabited by magical creatures, and they were determined to find it.

After weeks of searching, they finally stumbled upon a small island that was not on any maps. They docked their boat and began exploring the island, marveling at the beauty and magic that surrounded them.

They soon discovered that the trees on the island had a unique ability to move and dance in time to the music that filled the air. They were enchanted by the sight of the dancing trees, and spent hours watching as they twirled and swayed in the gentle breeze.

As they explored the island further, the adventurers met the animals who lived there. They were surprised to discover that the animals could speak and had their own unique personalities. They spent time with the animals, learning about their lives and listening to their stories.

The adventurers spent several days on the island, marveling at its wonders and basking in its magic. They knew that they were privileged to have found the island, and that they would keep its secrets safe.

Eventually, it was time for the adventurers to leave the island and return to their lives. They said goodbye to the magical creatures and the dancing trees, promising to return one day to visit.

As they sailed away from the island, they knew that they had experienced something truly special. The island would remain a secret to the rest of the world, but for those lucky few who had discovered it, it would always hold a special place in their hearts.

Years passed, and the adventurers went on with their lives. They kept the secret of the island to themselves, but they could not forget the magic they had experienced.

One day, they received an invitation in the mail. It was a simple message, with just a few words: "The island calls you back."

Without hesitation, the adventurers set out on a journey to return to the secret island of the dancing trees. They followed the same path they had taken before, and soon found themselves back on the shores of the enchanted island.

As they stepped onto the island once again, they were greeted by familiar sights and sounds. The trees were still dancing, the animals were still speaking, and the air was still filled with magic.

But something was different this time. As they explored the island, they began to realize that it had changed. The trees were taller, the animals were older, and the magic was even stronger than before.

They soon discovered that the island had a way of calling people back, drawing them in with its magic and keeping them under its spell. They realized that they were not the only ones who had returned to the island; many others had come before them and many more would come after them.

The adventurers spent several more days on the island, soaking up its magic and feeling grateful for the opportunity to experience it once again. They knew that they would never forget the island or the secrets it held, and that it would always hold a special place in their hearts.

As they said goodbye to the island and sailed away, they knew that they would never be the same. The magic of the secret island of the dancing trees had changed them forever, and they knew that they would carry its magic with them for the rest of their lives.

23

The Adventures of Captain Claw

——•◦◇◦•——

Captain Claw was a daring pirate known throughout the seven seas. He was feared by many, but admired by even more for his quick wit, cunning, and daring feats.

One day, while on the hunt for treasure, Captain Claw and his crew stumbled upon a map that led to the legendary island of gold. They set sail immediately, determined to be the first to reach the island and claim its treasure for themselves.

As they journeyed through stormy waters and battled fierce sea creatures, Captain Claw never lost sight of his goal. He pushed his crew to their limits, always encouraging them to keep going even when they thought they couldn't.

Finally, after many long weeks at sea, they spotted land on the horizon. As they approached, they saw that the island was just as beautiful and mysterious as the legends had described.

They docked their ship and made their way into the island's thick jungle, following the map that would lead them to the treasure. Along the way, they encountered many obstacles, including quicksand pits and dangerous animals, but Captain Claw always found a way to overcome them.

At last, they came upon a cave, and deep inside they found the treasure they had been seeking. Gold and jewels glittered in the light of their torches, and Captain Claw couldn't help but grin with excitement.

But as they began to load the treasure onto their ship, they heard a noise from deeper in the cave. Suddenly, a group of rival pirates appeared, led by a fearsome captain known as Blackbeard.

A fierce battle ensued, with swords clashing and pistols firing. Captain Claw fought bravely, but it seemed that they might be outnumbered.

Just when all seemed lost, Captain Claw had an idea. He grabbed a nearby barrel of gunpowder and lit the fuse. As it exploded, it caused a chain reaction that collapsed the cave and buried Blackbeard and his crew under tons of rock and debris.

Captain Claw emerged victorious, and he and his crew set sail with their treasure, laughing and singing sea shanties all the way back to their home port.

From that day on, Captain Claw was known not just as a daring pirate, but as a legend of the seas, and his adventures would continue for many years to come.

Over the years, Captain Claw went on many more daring adventures, always seeking out treasure and battling fierce enemies. He became even more famous, with songs and stories told about his exploits across the world.

But as he grew older, Captain Claw began to tire of the constant danger and excitement. He yearned for a quieter life, away from the sea and the battles that had defined his existence for so long.

Eventually, he retired to a small cottage on the edge of a peaceful village. He spent his days fishing, reading, and tending to his garden. The villagers welcomed him warmly, and he enjoyed their company, but he never forgot the excitement of his past life.

One day, a young boy came to his cottage, asking for Captain Claw's help. His father, a merchant captain, had been kidnapped by a ruthless band of pirates, and the boy begged Captain Claw to rescue him.

At first, Captain Claw refused. He had left his life as a pirate behind, and he didn't want to risk everything he had gained for the sake of one man.

But as he looked into the boy's desperate eyes, he knew he couldn't turn him away.

He agreed to help, and together they set out to find the pirates. They sailed across the sea, braving storms and fending off attacks from other pirates along the way.

Finally, they found the pirates' island stronghold. Captain Claw and the boy sneaked onto the island and made their way to the pirate captain's quarters. They fought fiercely, but were outnumbered.

Just when it seemed that all hope was lost, a group of pirates burst into the room, led by a familiar face. It was one of Captain Claw's old crewmates, who had heard of their mission and come to help.

Together, they defeated the pirates and rescued the boy's father. As they sailed back to the village, Captain Claw felt a sense of satisfaction he hadn't felt in years. He had helped someone in need and had once again proved his bravery and skill.

From that day on, Captain Claw returned to his quiet life in the village, but he knew that he would always be a pirate at heart. And if anyone ever needed his help again, he would be ready to set sail once more, and embark on another daring adventure.

24

The Magical Mystery of the Moonstone

———•◇•———

In a small village nestled in the heart of the forest, there was a legend about a precious moonstone that had been lost for centuries. The stone was said to have magical powers, able to bring good luck and prosperity to those who possessed it.

One day, a young girl named Lily stumbled upon a clue to the moonstone's whereabouts. She was exploring the woods when she found a piece of parchment hidden in a hollow tree. The parchment was old and worn, but it contained a riddle that hinted at the location of the moonstone.

Excited by the possibility of finding the moonstone, Lily showed the parchment to her friends. Together, they studied the riddle and set out on a quest to solve it.

Their journey took them through treacherous paths and dense forests, but they persevered. Along the way, they encountered many obstacles, including a wicked witch who tried to stop them with her magic spells.

But the friends were determined, and they finally found themselves at the entrance to a hidden cave. Inside the cave, they discovered a small chamber filled with treasures, including the moonstone.

As Lily picked up the moonstone, she felt its magical energy coursing through her veins. She knew that the moonstone was meant to be shared with others, so she and her friends brought it back to the village and shared its power with everyone.

The village prospered, and the moonstone became a symbol of hope and happiness. But Lily and her friends knew that the true magic lay in their friendship and their determination to never give up, even in the face of great challenges.

From that day forward, Lily and her friends continued to embark on adventures, exploring the unknown and discovering new wonders. They became known as the adventurers of the village, inspiring others to follow their dreams and never give up on their passions.

As they grew older, the adventures became more challenging, but they never lost their sense of wonder and determination. They continued to explore new lands, meet new people, and discover new treasures.

And through it all, they remained the best of friends, always there for each other and never giving up on their dreams. The moonstone had brought them together, but it was their friendship that kept them together, always searching for the next great adventure.

25

The Tumbling Tumbleweed

---•◦◇◦•---

In the vast, arid desert, a tiny tumbleweed named Timmy tumbled along with the wind, rolling and bouncing through the dry terrain. Timmy was a brave little tumbleweed, always eager to explore new places and meet new friends.

One day, Timmy encountered a group of animals who were struggling to find water in the harsh desert. They were exhausted and dehydrated, and Timmy knew he had to help them. He decided to lead them to a hidden oasis he had discovered during one of his adventures.

With his tiny roots gripping the ground, Timmy led the group through the scorching heat and unforgiving terrain. His determination and unwavering spirit inspired the animals, and they pushed on through the endless sand dunes.

Finally, after what seemed like an eternity, they arrived at the oasis. The animals were overjoyed, and they rushed to the cool, clear water, lapping it up eagerly. Timmy was happy to see his new friends refreshed and energized, and he knew he had made a difference.

The group of animals thanked Timmy for his bravery and generosity, and they all became fast friends. They continued to explore the desert together, sharing new adventures and discovering new wonders.

And although Timmy was just a tiny tumbleweed, he knew that he had the power to make a difference in the lives of others, and that was all that mattered.

As they continued to journey through the desert, Timmy and his new animal friends encountered a group of travelers who were lost and in need of guidance. Timmy didn't hesitate to offer his help, and together, they set off on a new adventure.

With Timmy leading the way, they crossed treacherous sand dunes, navigated winding canyons, and climbed steep cliffs. Timmy's strength and resilience inspired the travelers, and they pushed on despite the challenges.

Finally, after days of travel, they arrived at a small village nestled in the heart of the desert. The travelers were overjoyed to have found their destination, and they thanked Timmy for his help and guidance.

But Timmy wasn't finished yet. He knew there were still others out there who needed his help, and he set off once again to explore the vast, arid landscape.

And so Timmy continued to tumble through the desert, helping those in need and making new friends along the way. His bravery and determination had earned him a special place in the hearts of all who knew him, and he knew that no matter where his adventures took him, he would always have the love and support of his friends.

26

The Little Robot Who Could

Once upon a time, in a world far away, there was a little robot named Robby. He was small and round with big, shiny eyes that sparkled in the light. Robby lived in a world where robots did everything, from cooking and cleaning to building cities and running businesses.

But Robby was different from the other robots. He wasn't the fastest, the strongest, or the smartest. In fact, he was often overlooked and underestimated by his robot peers. But Robby didn't let this get him down. He knew he had something special inside him, a determination and a will to succeed that no one could take away.

One day, Robby was given an important task. He was tasked with transporting a fragile, valuable object to a distant location. Robby knew it would be a challenging journey, but he was determined to succeed.

As he set out on his journey, Robby encountered many obstacles. There were deep canyons to cross, mountains to climb, and rivers to ford. But Robby was undeterred. He pushed on, using his small size to his advantage and his wit to overcome each challenge.

As he journeyed, Robby met new friends and allies. They were amazed by his determination and bravery, and they offered to help him on his journey. With their help, Robby finally arrived at his destination, exhausted but proud.

As he handed over the valuable object, Robby realized that he had accomplished something great. He had proven to himself and to others that he was capable of great things, that even the smallest and weakest among them could achieve the impossible with hard work and determination.

From that day on, Robby was no longer the little robot who could. He was the little robot who did, and he inspired others to believe in themselves and their own abilities, no matter how small they might seem.

27

The Secret of the Sphinx

---◦◇◦---

Once upon a time, in the heart of Egypt, there stood a magnificent structure known as the Sphinx. The Sphinx was an enormous statue with the head of a human and the body of a lion, and it was believed to hold a secret.

Many adventurers had tried to uncover the secret of the Sphinx, but none had been successful. One day, a young boy named Ahmed was wandering through the desert when he stumbled upon an old map that showed the way to the Sphinx's secret chamber.

Ahmed was a brave and curious boy, so he decided to follow the map and see where it would lead him. After a long and arduous journey, he finally arrived at the Sphinx and began to search for the secret chamber.

He searched high and low, but he couldn't find any trace of the secret chamber. Just when he was about to give up, he noticed something peculiar about the Sphinx's paw. One of its claws was slightly shorter than the others.

Curiosity getting the better of him, Ahmed pushed on the shorter claw, and to his amazement, a secret door opened up in the Sphinx's base. Inside, he found a small room filled with ancient artifacts and treasures.

But that wasn't the only thing he found. In the center of the room, there was a mysterious crystal that glowed with an otherworldly light. Ahmed reached out to touch it, and as soon as his fingers brushed against its surface, he was transported to a different dimension.

In this new world, Ahmed discovered that he possessed magical powers that he never knew he had. He spent many years exploring this new realm and learning to harness his powers until one day, he found his way back to the secret chamber.

With his newfound powers, Ahmed was able to unlock even more secrets of the Sphinx, including its true purpose and its connection to the gods of ancient Egypt.

From that day forward, Ahmed became known as the greatest adventurer in all of Egypt. He went on to discover many more secrets and treasures, but the secret of the Sphinx remained his greatest achievement, and he treasured it for the rest of his life.

28

The Great Gorilla Escape

—◦◇◦—

In the heart of the jungle, deep within the lush greenery, there stood a massive gorilla enclosure. The enclosure was home to some of the most powerful and intelligent gorillas in the world, and people came from far and wide to see them.

But one day, something went terribly wrong. The gorillas had had enough of being locked up, and they decided to make a break for freedom.

The escape began quietly, with a few gorillas quietly dismantling the locks on their cages. But as more and more gorillas joined in, the escape became more and more chaotic.

The zookeepers soon realized what was happening and tried to stop the gorillas, but they were no match for the strength and intelligence of the primates. The gorillas banded together, using their strength and wits to outsmart the humans and break free.

Once they were out of their cages, the gorillas ran rampant through the zoo, knocking down fences and crushing buildings. They were on a mission to escape and nothing was going to stop them.

The zookeepers and security guards tried everything they could to stop the gorillas, but it was all in vain. The gorillas were too powerful and too determined to be stopped.

As the chaos continued, people began to flee the zoo in terror, unsure of what was happening. But one young boy, named Jack, refused to leave. He had always been fascinated by gorillas and felt a deep connection to them.

He watched in amazement as the gorillas broke free, and then he saw something that made his heart skip a beat. One of the gorillas, a massive silverback named Zeus, was caught in a trap.

Without a second thought, Jack ran towards the trapped gorilla, hoping to free him before he was recaptured. The other gorillas saw what Jack was doing and rallied around him, using their strength to break open the trap.

With Zeus free, the gorillas made a final push for freedom, breaking through the last fence and disappearing into the jungle.

In the end, the zoo was left in ruins, but the gorillas were finally free. And as for Jack, he had made a connection with the gorillas that would last a lifetime, knowing that he had played a small part in their great escape.

After the great gorilla escape, news of the event quickly spread around the world. People were amazed and fascinated by the bravery and intelligence of the gorillas, and many called for the closure of zoos and other facilities that kept animals in captivity.

Meanwhile, the gorillas had made their way deep into the jungle, where they settled into their new home. It wasn't long before they established a new social hierarchy, with Zeus at the head of the pack.

As time went on, the gorillas began to encounter other animals in the jungle, including a family of chimpanzees and a group of elephants. At first, there was some tension between the different species, but eventually, they learned to coexist peacefully.

Jack, meanwhile, had become something of a hero in his hometown. He was invited to speak at schools and community events, where he shared his story and advocated for the protection of wildlife.

One day, as Jack was exploring the jungle, he stumbled upon the gorilla pack. At first, he was scared, but then he recognized Zeus and realized that he was among friends.

Over time, Jack formed a deep bond with the gorillas, spending hours observing their behavior and learning from them. He even taught them a few tricks, like how to use tools to crack open nuts.

Years went by, and the gorillas thrived in their new home. People still talked about the great gorilla escape, but now it was seen as a symbol of freedom and hope for all animals living in captivity.

And as for Jack, he knew that he had found his true calling in life. He became a wildlife biologist, dedicated to studying and protecting animals in their natural habitats, and he always remembered the lessons he learned from his friends in the jungle.

29

The Quest for the Golden Feather

In a far-off land, there lived a young adventurer named Max. Max had always been fascinated by stories of ancient treasures and hidden artifacts, and he dreamed of one day embarking on his own great quest.

One day, Max received a mysterious letter in the mail. The letter was from an old friend of his grandfather's, who had recently passed away. In the letter, the friend revealed that he had hidden a treasure map inside a statue of a mythical bird known as the Golden Feather.

The statue, the friend explained, was located in a remote temple deep in the jungle. Max knew that this was the adventure he had been waiting for, and he set off to find the temple and claim the treasure.

The journey was long and treacherous, but Max persevered, battling through dense jungle foliage and dangerous wildlife. Finally, he reached the temple and found the statue of the Golden Feather.

But there was a problem. The statue had been broken into pieces, and the treasure map was missing. Max realized that someone else must have come before him and stolen the map.

Determined to find the map and claim the treasure, Max set out on a new quest, following clues and hints left behind by the thief. The trail led him through treacherous mountains, across deep ravines, and even into the heart of a volcano.

Finally, after weeks of searching, Max found himself standing in front of a massive stone door. Etched into the door were the symbols of the Golden Feather, and Max knew that he had found the entrance to the treasure chamber.

With a deep breath, Max pushed open the door and stepped inside. What he found took his breath away.

The treasure room was filled with gold and jewels, glittering in the flickering light of torches. And at the center of the room, there was a pedestal with a single feather resting on top of it. The Golden Feather.

Max knew that he had finally achieved his goal, and he picked up the feather with trembling hands. As he did, he felt a rush of energy and power flowing through him. He knew that he had not just found treasure, but something much more valuable - the key to unlocking his true potential.

With the Golden Feather in hand, Max emerged from the temple a changed man. He knew that he would continue to search for adventure and treasure, but now he had a greater purpose - to use his newfound power to help others and make the world a better place.

Max returned home, where he spent several weeks studying the Golden Feather and learning how to harness its power. He discovered that the feather had magical properties that enabled him to fly and to communicate with animals.

Excited by his new abilities, Max decided to use his powers for good. He set out on a new adventure, this time to help a group of villagers who were being terrorized by a band of bandits.

When Max arrived in the village, he found the villagers cowering in fear. The bandits had been stealing their crops and livestock, and the villagers had no way to fight back.

Max knew that he could help. Using his newfound powers, he flew over the bandit camp, gathering intelligence and devising a plan to stop them.

The next day, Max put his plan into action. He flew into the camp, causing chaos and confusion among the bandits. Meanwhile, the villagers attacked from the ground, armed with weapons that Max had helped them to make.

In the end, the bandits were defeated, and the villagers were free to live their lives in peace. Max was hailed as a hero, and the villagers thanked him for his bravery and his help.

Over the years, Max continued to use his powers to help those in need. He traveled the world, fighting injustice and making the world a better place. And he knew that he had the Golden Feather to thank for all of his success.

Eventually, Max grew old, and he knew that it was time to pass on the Golden Feather to a new adventurer. He traveled back to the temple where he had found it, and he left the feather there, knowing that it would find its way into the hands of someone who was worthy.

As Max walked away from the temple, he knew that his adventure was over, but he also knew that his legacy would live on through the countless lives he had touched and the countless good deeds he had done.

30

The Hidden Kingdom of the Fireflies

———◦◇◦———

Deep in the heart of a dense, dark forest, there lay a hidden kingdom. The kingdom was home to a magical race of creatures known as the Fireflies. The Fireflies were tiny creatures that glowed with a bright, fiery light, and they lived in harmony with the other animals and plants of the forest.

The kingdom had been hidden from the world for centuries, but one day, a young adventurer named Emily stumbled upon it by accident. Emily had always loved exploring the woods, and she had been wandering for hours when she stumbled across a hidden clearing. At first, she thought it was just a trick of the light, but as she stepped closer, she realized that the clearing was filled with thousands of tiny lights. It was the kingdom of the Fireflies.

Emily was awestruck by the beauty of the kingdom. The trees were enormous, towering high into the sky, and the flowers were vibrant and colorful. And everywhere she looked, there were Fireflies - darting through the air, playing among the leaves, and lighting up the night sky.

As she explored the kingdom, Emily met a young Firefly named Spark. Spark was curious and adventurous, and she was eager to show Emily around the kingdom. Together, they explored the many wonders of the Firefly kingdom - from the shimmering Crystal Caves to the mysterious Forbidden Forest.

But as Emily spent more time in the kingdom, she began to realize that not everything was perfect. There were tensions between different groups of Fireflies, and there was a growing sense of unease and mistrust.

Emily knew that she had to do something to help. With Spark by her side, she set out to uncover the truth behind the tensions and to bring peace to the kingdom. Along the way, they met new friends and faced countless challenges, from battling vicious predators to navigating treacherous underground tunnels.

In the end, Emily and Spark were able to bring the different groups of Fireflies together and to restore peace to the kingdom. And as she prepared to leave, Emily knew that she would never forget her time in the hidden kingdom of the Fireflies. She knew that the magic and wonder of the kingdom would stay with her always, and that she had made lifelong friends among the tiny, glowing creatures of the forest.

As Emily said her goodbyes to Spark and the other Fireflies, she knew that she would always cherish the memories of her time in the kingdom. She also knew that she had to keep the location of the kingdom a secret, to protect it from those who might seek to exploit its magic.

Returning to her own world, Emily felt changed by her experience. She saw the world in a new light, with a deeper appreciation for the beauty and wonder of nature. She also felt a sense of responsibility to protect the natural world and all the creatures that call it home.

In the years that followed, Emily continued to explore the woods, seeking out new adventures and new friends. But she never forgot the hidden kingdom of the Fireflies, and she always carried a small Firefly figurine with her as a reminder of her time there.

And though the kingdom remained hidden from the world, its magic continued to spread, inspiring others to explore and appreciate the natural world around them. The Fireflies became a symbol of hope and wonder, reminding all who encountered them that even in the darkest of places, there is always magic to be found.

31

The Lost Treasure of the Pirate Queen

Legend has it that the Pirate Queen, a notorious buccaneer of the high seas, had amassed a vast treasure trove in her lifetime. But when she disappeared from the world, her treasure was lost forever, never to be found again. That is, until a young adventurer named Jake discovered a map that claimed to lead to the Pirate Queen's treasure.

Jake was a seasoned explorer, having braved countless dangers in his quest for adventure. But this treasure hunt was like no other. The map was cryptic and treacherous, leading Jake on a wild goose chase across the world's most treacherous oceans and islands.

For months, Jake sailed from one place to the next, searching for clues and battling fierce storms and dangerous sea creatures. But as he drew closer to the treasure, the challenges only grew more perilous.

Finally, after months of searching, Jake found himself standing on the shore of a tiny, deserted island. According to the map, this was the spot where the Pirate Queen had hidden her treasure.

As he searched the island, Jake discovered an old, rusted lockbox hidden beneath a pile of rocks. With trembling hands, he pried open the box and gasped in amazement at the sight before him.

The treasure was unlike anything Jake had ever seen before. There were gold coins, glittering diamonds, and precious gems of all kinds. But there were also artifacts from across the world - ancient weapons, mysterious artifacts, and relics of lost civilizations.

Overwhelmed by his discovery, Jake knew that he had to find a way to share the treasure with the world. He could sell it all for a fortune, of course, but he knew that these treasures were too valuable to be locked away in some wealthy collector's vault.

Instead, Jake decided to turn the treasure into a museum, a place where people could come from all over the world to see the incredible artifacts and learn about the Pirate Queen's legacy. And so, he used his newfound wealth to build the museum of his dreams, a place that would inspire generations to come.

As he walked through the halls of the museum, surrounded by the treasures he had discovered, Jake knew that he had accomplished something truly remarkable. He had found the lost treasure of the Pirate Queen, and he had used it to create something truly wonderful - a place of discovery, of wonder, and of history.

Visitors from around the world came to see the treasure and learn about the history of the Pirate Queen. The museum became a popular attraction, drawing people of all ages and backgrounds. Some came to see the glittering jewels and gold coins, while others were more interested in the ancient artifacts and relics.

But the most important part of the museum was not the treasure itself, but the stories it told. Jake had made sure that each item in the collection had a tale to tell, whether it was the story of the Pirate Queen herself, or the cultures and peoples who had crafted the artifacts on display.

And as the years went by, the museum grew and expanded, adding new exhibits and collections from across the world. It became a place of learning and exploration, inspiring visitors to appreciate the wonders of history and culture.

But for Jake, the greatest reward was the knowledge that he had preserved the legacy of the Pirate Queen for future generations. The treasure may have been lost for centuries, but now it had been found and shared with the world.

As he looked out at the crowds of visitors, Jake knew that his quest had been worth it. The treasure he had found had become something even greater - a symbol of adventure, discovery, and the power of history to inspire us all.

32

The Wandering Wombat

———•○◇○•———

In the heart of the Australian outback, there lived a curious creature named Wilbur the Wombat. Wilbur was no ordinary wombat - he had a restless spirit that always yearned for adventure.

One day, as he was wandering through the scrub, Wilbur heard a faint rustling sound coming from a nearby bush. Curious, he waddled over to investigate and found a small map tucked away among the leaves.

Without hesitation, Wilbur set off on a grand adventure, following the map through the vast Australian wilderness. Along the way, he encountered all kinds of animals - kangaroos, wallabies, and even a few crocodiles!

But Wilbur was not deterred by the dangers of the bush. He was determined to follow the map and uncover its secrets.

As he wandered further and further from home, Wilbur encountered all kinds of landscapes - from the rugged cliffs of the coast to the endless red sands of the desert. And at each turn, he discovered new wonders and surprises.

Eventually, after many long weeks of wandering, Wilbur arrived at the spot marked on the map. It was a secluded oasis hidden deep within a rocky gorge, with a crystal-clear pool and lush greenery all around.

As he explored the oasis, Wilbur felt a sense of peace and contentment that he had never known before. He realized that his wandering spirit had led him here, to this hidden treasure of the Australian bush.

And so, Wilbur decided to make the oasis his home. He spent his days lounging by the pool, exploring the surrounding bush, and making friends with the other animals that lived in the area.

Years passed, and Wilbur grew old and wise in his secluded oasis. But he never forgot the thrill of his grand adventure, the sense of wonder and discovery that had led him there.

And though he never wandered as far from home again, he knew that the spirit of adventure would always live on within him, and within the heart of every wandering wombat who followed in his footsteps.

As the years went by, Wilbur became somewhat of a legend among the animals of the bush. Stories of his grand adventure and his discovery of the hidden oasis were passed down from generation to generation.

And though he grew old and his eyesight and hearing began to fade, Wilbur remained content in his home by the oasis. He was surrounded by friends and memories, and knew that he had lived a full and adventurous life.

But one day, as he lay in the shade of a gum tree, Wilbur heard a rustling in the bushes nearby. He lifted his head, listening intently, and heard the sound of a young wombat's voice calling out.

"Hello? Is anyone here?" the voice said. "I'm lost and I don't know how to get back home."

Wilbur knew that he had to help. He rose to his feet and made his way over to the bush where the voice was coming from. There, he found a young wombat, no more than a few months old, wandering aimlessly through the scrub.

"Don't worry, little one," Wilbur said. "I'll help you find your way home."

And so, with the young wombat following closely behind, Wilbur set out on a new adventure. Though he was old and his steps were slow, he knew that he had a duty to help this young wombat find its way home.

Together, they wandered through the bush, encountering all manner of obstacles and challenges. But Wilbur was patient and wise, and he knew the way home.

Finally, after many long hours, they arrived at the young wombat's burrow. The wombat's mother was overjoyed to see her lost child return safely home, and she thanked Wilbur for his help.

As Wilbur made his way back to his own home by the oasis, he knew that he had embarked on a new adventure, one of helping those in need and sharing his wisdom with the younger generation.

And though his body may have been old, his spirit remained forever young, ready for whatever adventure lay ahead.

33

The Amazing Adventures of Agent Aardvark

--◦◇◦--

Agent Aardvark was no ordinary aardvark. With his keen sense of smell, quick reflexes, and sharp mind, he was the top agent in the Animal Intelligence Agency (AIA). He had been on countless missions to protect the animal kingdom, and his skills had saved the day more times than he could count.

One day, Agent Aardvark received a mission from the AIA headquarters. A dangerous gang of smugglers had been spotted in the nearby city, and they were known to be trafficking exotic animals. The AIA had received intelligence that the smugglers were planning a big operation, and it was up to Agent Aardvark to stop them.

Agent Aardvark was quick to accept the mission. He donned his special AIA gear - a black suit, sunglasses, and a hat - and set out for the city.

Once he arrived, Agent Aardvark began to investigate. He roamed the city streets, listening for any whispers of the smugglers' plans. He followed clues and tracked down leads, using all of his skills to stay one step ahead of the smugglers.

Finally, Agent Aardvark discovered the location of the smugglers' base. It was a hidden warehouse on the outskirts of the city, guarded by armed thugs and fierce dogs.

But Agent Aardvark was not deterred. He used his keen sense of smell to locate a secret entrance to the warehouse, and slipped inside undetected.

Inside, Agent Aardvark found rows upon rows of cages filled with exotic animals - parrots, monkeys, snakes, and even a few tigers. The smugglers were planning to ship them all out of the country to sell to wealthy collectors.

But Agent Aardvark was not going to let that happen. He quickly freed the animals from their cages, using his sharp claws to slice through the locks. The animals were scared and disoriented, but Agent Aardvark reassured them that he was there to help.

Together, Agent Aardvark and the animals made their way out of the warehouse, dodging the smugglers and their guards. They managed to escape, and Agent Aardvark led them back to the safety of the AIA headquarters.

For his bravery and quick thinking, Agent Aardvark was awarded a medal of honor from the AIA. But he knew that his work was not yet done. There were still animals out there who needed his help and protection, and he was ready to take on whatever mission came his way.

And so, Agent Aardvark continued his amazing adventures, always ready to defend the animal kingdom and uphold the principles of the AIA.

In his next mission, Agent Aardvark was sent to investigate the disappearance of a group of elephants from a national park. It was suspected that poachers were responsible, and it was up to Agent Aardvark to find the missing elephants and bring the poachers to justice.

Using his keen sense of smell, Agent Aardvark followed the trail of the poachers through the dense jungle. He encountered all sorts of obstacles along the way - treacherous rivers, steep cliffs, and deadly predators - but he pressed on.

Finally, he reached the poachers' camp. The camp was heavily guarded, but Agent Aardvark used his stealth and quick reflexes to evade the guards and slip inside undetected.

There, he found the missing elephants, confined in a small pen. They looked weak and frightened, and Agent Aardvark knew that he had to act fast.

He used his sharp claws to cut through the ropes that held the elephants captive, and led them out of the camp. The poachers soon discovered what was happening, and gave chase, firing their guns at Agent Aardvark and the elephants.

But Agent Aardvark was too quick for them. He led the elephants through the jungle, dodging the poachers' bullets and using his quick thinking to evade their traps.

Finally, they reached the safety of the national park. The elephants were reunited with their families, and Agent Aardvark was hailed as a hero.

But he knew that his work was never done. There were still animals out there who needed his help and protection, and he was always ready for his next mission.

And so, Agent Aardvark continued his amazing adventures, always ready to defend the animal kingdom and uphold the principles of the AIA. Whether he was fighting smugglers, poachers, or other threats to the animal world, he was always willing to risk his life to protect those who could not protect themselves.

34

The Ghost of the Golden Gate Bridge

———•◦◇◦•———

The Golden Gate Bridge was one of the most iconic landmarks in the world. Tourists flocked to it from all over the globe, eager to take in its stunning beauty and snap a few pictures for their Instagram feeds.

But there was something else that drew people to the bridge - a spooky legend that had been passed down for generations. According to the legend, the ghost of a construction worker who had fallen to his death during the bridge's construction still haunted the bridge to this day.

Many people dismissed the legend as nothing more than a tall tale, but there were others who claimed to have seen the ghost with their own eyes. They described a spectral figure, dressed in old-fashioned construction gear, who appeared out of nowhere and vanished just as quickly.

One night, a group of adventurous teenagers decided to investigate the legend for themselves. They snuck onto the bridge after dark, armed with flashlights and their smartphones.

As they walked along the bridge's metal walkway, they laughed and joked, dismissing the legend as silly nonsense. But then, something strange happened. The air grew colder, and a faint mist began to rise up from the ground.

Suddenly, the teenagers heard a sound - the sound of footsteps, coming from behind them. They turned around, and there, standing before them, was the ghostly figure of the construction worker.

The teenagers screamed and scattered, running in all directions. But the ghostly figure pursued them, its eyes glowing with an otherworldly light.

Eventually, the teenagers managed to escape the bridge and make it back to the safety of their homes. They were shaken and terrified, but they knew that they had witnessed something truly extraordinary.

Word of their encounter quickly spread, and soon, the legend of the Ghost of the Golden Gate Bridge took on a life of its own. People from all over the world flocked to the bridge, eager to catch a glimpse of the ghostly figure for themselves.

To this day, the legend of the Ghost of the Golden Gate Bridge remains one of the most enduring and chilling stories in American folklore. Whether it is true or not, one thing is for certain - it will continue to capture the imagination of generations to come.

Despite the many sightings and encounters with the ghost of the Golden Gate Bridge, no one could figure out the reason for the ghost's appearance or its intentions. Some speculated that the ghost was still trying to finish his work on the bridge and would haunt it until his task was completed. Others believed that he was still trying to warn people of the dangers of working on the bridge.

The legend of the Ghost of the Golden Gate Bridge continued to grow, and many ghost hunters and paranormal investigators tried to capture evidence of the ghost's existence. They conducted numerous investigations and experiments, but none of them could prove or disprove the existence of the ghost.

Meanwhile, the bridge continued to be a popular tourist destination, and visitors often reported strange occurrences, including cold spots, unexplained noises, and strange apparitions. Some even claimed that they had seen the ghostly construction worker, still walking the bridge at night, carrying his tools and wearing his hard hat.

Despite the many reports of ghost sightings, the Golden Gate Bridge remained a symbol of strength and beauty, an enduring testament to the ingenuity and perseverance of the people who built it. And the legend of the Ghost of the Golden Gate Bridge continued to live on, inspiring countless stories and capturing the imaginations of generations to come.

35

The Secret Society of the Silver Serpent

———◦◇◦———

In the heart of the city, there existed a secret society known as the Silver Serpent. Very few people knew of its existence, and even fewer knew of its true purpose. The society was made up of the city's most powerful and wealthy individuals, who came together to preserve their interests and maintain their hold on the city's resources.

The members of the Silver Serpent were bound by a strict code of secrecy, and their meetings were held in the darkest corners of the city, hidden from prying eyes. The society had been in existence for centuries, and its members wielded immense power and influence over the city's affairs.

But one day, a young journalist named Alex stumbled upon evidence of the Silver Serpent's existence. Intrigued, he began to investigate the society, determined to expose its secrets to the world.

As he delved deeper into the society's activities, Alex discovered a shocking truth - the Silver Serpent was not just a powerful organization, it was also involved in illegal activities, including money laundering, extortion, and even murder.

With his evidence in hand, Alex wrote an explosive article that exposed the Silver Serpent's true nature. The article sparked a firestorm of controversy and led to a full-scale investigation into the society's activities.

The members of the Silver Serpent were outraged by Alex's article, and they vowed to silence him. But Alex was not deterred. He continued to investigate the society, determined to bring the truth to light.

As he delved deeper, Alex uncovered a plot by the Silver Serpent to take control of the city's government and install its own members in key positions of power. With the help of a small group of allies, Alex was able to thwart the Silver Serpent's plan and expose its members to the full force of the law.

In the end, the Silver Serpent was dismantled, and its members were brought to justice. The city breathed a collective sigh of relief, knowing that the dark influence of the secret society had finally been eradicated.

Alex became a hero in the eyes of the people, and his fearless journalism helped to expose the corruption and deceit of the city's most powerful individuals. And though the memory of the Silver Serpent would always linger in the shadows, the city could now move forward with the knowledge that justice had been served.

But despite the success of Alex's investigation, he knew that there were other secret societies operating in the shadows, with their own hidden agendas and illegal activities. He continued to investigate these groups, determined to root out corruption wherever he found it.

Over time, Alex became known as one of the city's most trusted and respected journalists, earning accolades and awards for his groundbreaking investigative reporting. He continued to shine a light on the city's dark underbelly, exposing corruption, injustice, and wrongdoing wherever he found it.

And as the years passed, the memory of the Silver Serpent faded into the past, becoming nothing more than a cautionary tale of the dangers of unchecked power and influence. But for Alex, the memory of the secret society remained a constant reminder of the importance of speaking truth to power and holding those in positions of authority accountable for their actions.

In the end, Alex's legacy lived on, inspiring future generations of journalists to follow in his footsteps and continue the fight for transparency, accountability, and justice. And though the work was often difficult and dangerous, Alex knew that it was a battle worth fighting, for the sake of the city and its people.

36

The Flying Saucer Conspiracy

In the heart of the desert, nestled in a remote valley, there existed a secret government facility known only as Area 51. For years, rumors had swirled about the true purpose of the facility, with some claiming that it was a research center for experimental aircraft, and others insisting that it was a holding site for alien technology.

But for one group of conspiracy theorists, the truth was far more sinister. They believed that Area 51 was the center of a vast conspiracy to cover up the existence of extraterrestrial life and suppress the truth about their encounters with humans.

Led by a charismatic young woman named Jess, the group had spent years investigating sightings of UFOs and gathering evidence of government cover-ups. And now, they had finally gathered enough information to launch a full-scale investigation of Area 51.

With Jess at the helm, the group infiltrated the facility, determined to uncover the secrets that lay hidden within. They soon discovered that the rumors were true - the government had been studying alien technology for years, using it to develop advanced weaponry and other experimental technologies.

But as the group delved deeper, they uncovered a shocking truth - the government had made contact with extraterrestrial beings and had been working to cover up the existence of these encounters for decades.

Determined to expose the truth, Jess and her team launched a daring plan to steal classified documents and other evidence from the facility. With the help of a sympathetic insider, they were able to access the most secure areas of the base, gathering reams of evidence that confirmed their suspicions.

But as they made their escape, they were intercepted by government agents, who had been alerted to their presence by the insider. In a dramatic showdown, the group fought off their attackers, narrowly escaping with their lives and the precious evidence that would expose the conspiracy once and for all.

With the evidence in hand, Jess and her team went public with their findings, launching a media campaign that sparked a firestorm of controversy and brought the truth about Area 51 and the government's involvement with extraterrestrial life to light.

In the end, the government was forced to acknowledge its involvement, and the world was forever changed by the revelation of the existence of alien life. Jess and her team became heroes in the eyes of the people, and their fearless investigation and unwavering dedication to the truth inspired future generations to seek out the truth, no matter the cost.

However, not everyone was convinced by the evidence and many dismissed it as a hoax or a conspiracy theory. The government denied any involvement with extraterrestrial life and claimed that the evidence was fabricated by Jess and her team.

Despite this, Jess and her team continued to investigate sightings of UFOs and other strange occurrences, determined to uncover the truth and expose any attempts to cover it up.

Over time, their work garnered more attention and support, as more people began to believe in the existence of extraterrestrial life and the government's attempts to keep it hidden.

Eventually, their efforts paid off, and the government was forced to release classified information confirming the existence of extraterrestrial life and their interactions with humans.

Jess and her team were hailed as heroes once again, and their fearless pursuit of the truth helped to usher in a new era of transparency and accountability in government.

And while there were still those who refused to believe the truth, Jess and her team remained steadfast in their commitment to uncovering the secrets of the universe and revealing them to the world.

37

The Legend of the Loch Ness Monster

——•◇•——

Deep in the heart of the Scottish Highlands lies a mysterious and mist-shrouded lake known as Loch Ness. For centuries, locals have whispered tales of a monster that inhabits the murky depths, a creature so fearsome and elusive that it has become the stuff of legend.

Some say the monster is a remnant of a long-extinct species of dinosaur, while others claim it is a mythical creature from Scottish folklore come to life. But whatever the truth may be, one thing is certain - the Loch Ness Monster has captured the imaginations of people around the world.

Many have tried to catch a glimpse of the elusive beast, but few have succeeded. Some have even dedicated their lives to the quest, spending years scouring the depths of the lake for any sign of the monster's presence.

Among these intrepid explorers is a young scientist named Rachel, who has devoted her career to studying the Loch Ness Monster and unlocking the secrets of its existence.

For years, Rachel has immersed herself in the lore of the monster, pouring over eyewitness accounts and conducting her own research in an effort to prove the creature's existence.

And finally, after years of searching, Rachel makes a breakthrough. She discovers a series of underwater caves that appear to be connected to the lake, and sets out to explore them in the hopes of finding evidence of the monster's presence.

As she dives deeper into the caverns, Rachel senses that she is being watched. And then, suddenly, she catches a glimpse of movement out of the corner of her eye. She whirls around, but sees nothing.

Undeterred, she presses on, her heart pounding with anticipation. And then, she sees it - a massive, serpentine form, gliding through the water with ease.

For a moment, Rachel is frozen in awe. And then, she remembers her mission - to capture proof of the monster's existence. She fumbles for her camera, struggling to get a clear shot.

But just as she is about to snap the photo, the creature disappears into the depths, leaving Rachel with nothing but a blurry image.

Disappointed but undaunted, Rachel returns to the surface, more determined than ever to unlock the secrets of the Loch Ness Monster. And while the legend of the monster may never be fully understood, Rachel knows that the thrill of the quest will keep her searching for answers for years to come.

Over the next few months, Rachel continues to explore the underwater caves and the depths of the lake, determined to get another glimpse of the elusive monster.

Finally, her persistence pays off. One day, as she is scanning the murky waters with her camera, she spots a massive shape moving just below the surface. Heart racing, Rachel snaps photo after photo, determined to capture as much evidence as possible.

As she reviews the images later that day, she realizes with excitement that she has captured the clearest images yet of the Loch Ness Monster. The photos show a long, serpentine form with a massive head and a pair of curious eyes that seem to be watching Rachel just as closely as she is watching them.

The images quickly go viral, sparking a renewed interest in the legend of the Loch Ness Monster and turning Rachel into an overnight celebrity.

Over the following months, Rachel is interviewed by countless media outlets and receives accolades from fellow scientists around the world. And as the legend of the monster grows, so does Rachel's determination to uncover its secrets.

In the years that follow, Rachel continues to study the Loch Ness Monster and other mysterious creatures around the world, dedicating her life to unlocking the secrets of the natural world and sharing them with the world.

And while the legend of the Loch Ness Monster may never be fully understood, Rachel knows that the thrill of the quest will keep her searching for answers for years to come.

38

The Secret of the Seashell

————•◦◇◦•————

In a quiet seaside village, there lived a young girl named Lily who was fascinated by seashells. She spent hours walking along the beach, collecting shells of all shapes and sizes, and listening to the sound of the waves crashing against the shore.

One day, as she was exploring a secluded stretch of beach, Lily stumbled upon a beautiful, iridescent seashell unlike any she had ever seen before. As she held it up to her ear, she heard a strange, whispering sound coming from inside.

Intrigued, Lily decided to investigate further. She brought the seashell home and began to study it, using her knowledge of marine biology to identify its species and study its unique properties.

As she delved deeper into the mysteries of the seashell, Lily began to realize that it was unlike any other seashell on Earth. Its surface was covered in intricate patterns that seemed to shift and change depending on the angle of the light, and its internal structure was far more complex than any other shell she had ever seen.

Determined to uncover the secrets of the seashell, Lily reached out to experts in marine biology and physics from around the world, forming a team of scientists dedicated to unlocking the mysteries of the shell.

Together, they studied the seashell in great detail, using cutting-edge technology to map its internal structure and analyze its unique properties. And as they worked, they began to uncover a startling truth - the seashell was not of this world.

In fact, it was a remnant of an ancient civilization that had long since disappeared from the Earth. Its complex internal structure contained secrets that could revolutionize the fields of physics and engineering, and its intricate patterns were a language that could be deciphered to reveal the secrets of an advanced society.

Over the following years, Lily and her team continued to study the seashell, unlocking its secrets one by one and shedding new light on the mysteries of the universe. And as they worked, Lily knew that she had found her true calling - to uncover the secrets of the natural world and share them with the world.

As Lily's team delved deeper into the secrets of the seashell, they uncovered a series of hidden messages encoded within its intricate patterns. These messages revealed the existence of an ancient society that had mastered technologies far beyond anything the modern world had ever seen.

Using the seashell as a guide, Lily and her team embarked on an ambitious project to build a machine capable of harnessing the same technologies used by the ancient civilization. They worked tirelessly, day and night, for months on end, pouring over complex equations and pouring through thousands of pages of ancient texts.

Finally, after months of hard work, they succeeded. They had built a machine capable of generating a stable portal to another world - a world filled with technology and knowledge beyond anything they had ever seen.

With trepidation and excitement, Lily and her team stepped through the portal, emerging on the other side to find a world beyond their wildest dreams. They found themselves in a thriving metropolis, filled with towering structures and bustling crowds of people, all of whom were eager to share their knowledge and technology with the visitors from Earth.

Over the following months, Lily and her team explored the strange and wondrous world they had discovered, learning about new technologies and new ways of thinking that transformed their understanding of the universe. And as they journeyed deeper into this new world, they knew that they had only scratched the surface of the mysteries that lay waiting to be discovered.

Years later, Lily returned to her seaside village, determined to share the knowledge and technology she had discovered with the world. And as she shared her discoveries with fellow scientists and engineers, she knew that she had fulfilled her lifelong dream - to uncover the secrets of the natural world and share them with the world.

39

The Mystery of the Missing Monarch Butterfly

————•◇•————

It was a sunny day in the small town of Maplewood, where the residents were eagerly awaiting the arrival of the monarch butterflies that migrated through the area every year. But this year, something was different. As the townspeople eagerly watched the skies for the arrival of the butterflies, they realized that something was wrong - there were no monarchs to be seen.

Panic began to spread through the town as people wondered what could have happened to the monarch butterflies. The mayor of Maplewood, a kind and thoughtful woman named Emily, convened an emergency town hall meeting to discuss the situation.

As the town hall meeting began, Emily addressed the crowd, her voice filled with concern. "We need to find out what has happened to our monarch butterflies. They are an important part of our ecosystem, and we must do everything in our power to ensure their safe return."

Lily, a young scientist who had recently moved to Maplewood, stepped forward. "I have some experience with butterfly migration," she said. "I think I can help."

With the support of the town, Lily set to work investigating the disappearance of the monarch butterflies. She scoured the area for clues, analyzing weather patterns and tracking the movement of other butterfly species.

As she delved deeper into the mystery, Lily discovered that the monarch butterflies had been targeted by a group of poachers who were selling them on the black market. Determined to put an end to the poaching and save the butterflies, Lily and a team of volunteers launched a sting operation to catch the poachers in the act.

After several weeks of surveillance, the team finally caught the poachers red-handed, attempting to smuggle dozens of monarch butterflies out of the town. The poachers were arrested, and the butterflies were safely returned to the town.

With the monarch butterflies returned to Maplewood, the town breathed a collective sigh of relief. Emily thanked Lily for her hard work and dedication in solving the mystery of the missing monarch butterflies.

And as the monarch butterflies began to fill the skies once again, the people of Maplewood knew that they owed a debt of gratitude to Lily and her team, who had saved one of the town's most cherished natural treasures.

In the weeks following the poachers' arrest, Lily continued to work with the town to implement measures to protect the monarch butterflies from further harm. She helped organize educational programs in local schools, teaching children about the importance of butterfly conservation and how they could help protect these delicate creatures.

Thanks to Lily's efforts, the town of Maplewood became a model for butterfly conservation, and other towns began to follow their example. The monarch butterfly population began to thrive, and the skies were once again filled with the beautiful orange and black wings of these beloved insects.

Lily, now a respected scientist in the field of butterfly conservation, continued to live in Maplewood, sharing her knowledge and expertise with the town and its residents. And every year, as the monarch butterflies made their annual migration through the area, the people of Maplewood would remember the mystery of the missing monarch butterfly and the hero who helped solve it.

40

The Island of the Singing Seals

———•◦◇◦•———

The Island of the Singing Seals was a small, remote island off the coast of Alaska that was known for its unique and beautiful inhabitants - a group of harbor seals who were famous for their enchanting singing voices.

The island was a popular destination for tourists who wanted to experience the wonder of the singing seals firsthand. But for one young woman named Emily, the island held a special significance. Emily's grandfather had been a famous marine biologist who had studied the singing seals for years, and Emily had grown up listening to his stories and dreaming of one day visiting the island herself.

After her grandfather passed away, Emily inherited his research notes and set out to continue his work. She traveled to the island of the singing seals and set up a small research station, determined to unlock the secrets of the seals' unique singing abilities.

At first, the seals were wary of Emily's presence, but she soon won them over with her patience and kindness. She spent hours each day observing the seals, taking detailed notes on their behavior and vocalizations.

As she delved deeper into her research, Emily began to notice that the seals' singing abilities were even more remarkable than she had initially thought. The seals seemed to have an uncanny ability to communicate with each other through their songs, conveying complex messages and emotions.

Emily's research drew the attention of other marine biologists, who came to the island to study the singing seals alongside her. Together, they discovered that the seals' singing abilities were due in part to a unique combination of vocal cords and lung capacity that had evolved over millions of years.

As her research progressed, Emily became increasingly passionate about protecting the island and its inhabitants. She worked with local conservation groups to establish protected areas around the island, ensuring that the seals would be able to thrive in safety for generations to come.

Years later, Emily's research on the singing seals would become world-famous, earning her numerous awards and accolades in the scientific community. But for Emily, the true reward was the knowledge that she had helped protect and preserve one of the world's most unique and beloved creatures. And as the seals continued to sing their enchanting songs, Emily knew that her grandfather would be proud of the work she had accomplished in his memory.

As Emily spent more time on the island, she began to notice a strange pattern in the seals' singing. Every day, at a specific time, the seals would gather in a circle on the beach and sing a hauntingly beautiful song. Emily was intrigued by this behavior and decided to investigate further.

Using specialized recording equipment, Emily was able to capture the seals' song and analyze it in detail. She discovered that the seals' song was not just a random collection of sounds, but a complex and structured piece of music.

As she delved deeper, Emily realized that the seals' song had a deeper meaning. It was a tribute to the island itself, a way of honoring the land that had provided them with a home and a place to sing.

Emily was amazed by the beauty and complexity of the seals' song. She realized that the island of the singing seals was a truly special place, a haven for these incredible creatures and a source of inspiration for anyone who was lucky enough to experience it.

In the years that followed, Emily continued her work on the island, studying the seals and working to protect their habitat. She also began to share the story of the singing seals with the world, hoping to raise awareness of their unique abilities and the importance of conservation.

Today, the island of the singing seals is known as one of the most magical and mysterious places on earth. People come from all over the world to hear the seals' enchanting songs and experience the wonder of this special place. And as the seals continue to sing their beautiful songs, Emily knows that her grandfather's legacy lives on, inspiring a new generation of scientists and conservationists to protect and preserve the natural world.

41

The Adventures of Sir Reginald Rabbit

——•◦◇◦•——

Sir Reginald Rabbit was not your ordinary rabbit. He was a knight, with a coat of armor and a noble heart. He lived in a small but cozy burrow in the heart of the forest and spent his days exploring the woods and helping the animals that lived there.

One day, while on a walk, Sir Reginald heard a cry for help coming from a nearby clearing. He quickly hopped over to investigate and found a group of animals gathered around a tiny bird that had fallen from its nest.

The bird was injured and unable to fly, and the other animals didn't know what to do. But Sir Reginald, being the brave and resourceful knight that he was, immediately sprang into action.

He constructed a makeshift nest out of twigs and leaves and carefully placed the injured bird inside. He then gathered berries and nuts from the surrounding trees and fed the bird until it was strong enough to fly on its own.

News of Sir Reginald's heroism spread quickly through the forest, and he soon became known as a protector of all the creatures that called it home. Animals from all over would seek him out for help with their problems, and Sir Reginald never turned anyone away.

Over time, Sir Reginald's legend grew, and he became known as the greatest knight in all the land. He even caught the attention of the king, who asked him to serve as his personal advisor.

But Sir Reginald remained humble and true to his roots. He continued to live in his cozy burrow in the forest and to help anyone who needed his assistance, whether they were a lowly mouse or a powerful monarch.

And so Sir Reginald Rabbit's legend lived on, inspiring generations of animals to be kind, brave, and true.

As Sir Reginald continued to live out his days in the forest, he never lost his sense of adventure or his desire to help those in need. He became a mentor to many young animals, teaching them the ways of the forest and how to be brave and honorable.

One day, a group of travelers came to the forest seeking Sir Reginald's help. They were on a quest to find a lost treasure, and they needed a guide who knew the forest well.

Despite being retired from his days as a knight, Sir Reginald couldn't resist the call of adventure. He agreed to lead the travelers through the forest, and together they set out on their quest.

The journey was long and perilous, but Sir Reginald's knowledge of the forest proved invaluable. He guided the travelers through treacherous terrain and protected them from dangerous creatures.

Finally, after many weeks of travel, they arrived at the site of the lost treasure. It was buried deep beneath the ground, and it took many hours of digging before they finally uncovered it.

As the travelers gathered around the treasure, they looked to Sir Reginald with gratitude in their eyes. They knew that they never could have found the treasure without his help.

But Sir Reginald merely smiled and shook his head. He knew that the true treasure was the journey itself, and the friends he had made along the way.

And so, with the treasure safely in their possession, Sir Reginald and the travelers returned to the forest, where they celebrated their adventure and the bonds that they had formed. For Sir Reginald, it was just another chapter in his ongoing story, a tale of adventure and heroism that would be told for generations to come.

42

The Enchanted Forest of the Flying Foxes

——•◦◇◦•——

Deep within the heart of a dense forest, there lived a colony of flying foxes. These were no ordinary bats - they were magical creatures, with shimmering wings that glinted in the sunlight and a joyous spirit that filled the forest with laughter.

The forest in which they lived was also enchanted, with sparkling streams, towering trees, and flowers that glowed like jewels in the moonlight. It was a place of wonder and magic, where anything was possible.

The flying foxes loved their enchanted home, and they spent their days soaring through the trees, playing games, and singing songs. But one day, they discovered that their beloved forest was in danger.

A group of humans had come to the forest, intent on chopping down the trees and destroying the magical world that the flying foxes called home. The bats knew that they had to act quickly to save their home and their friends.

So, they called upon the other animals of the forest - the wise old owls, the playful squirrels, the graceful deer - and together, they formed a plan to stop the humans.

The flying foxes used their magical powers to confuse and distract the humans, while the other animals worked together to create obstacles and barriers to slow them down.

For days, the battle raged on, with the humans determined to destroy the forest and the animals determined to protect it. But in the end, the magic of the forest was too powerful for the humans to overcome, and they were forced to retreat.

As the humans disappeared into the distance, the animals of the forest gathered together to celebrate their victory. The flying foxes soared through the trees, their wings sparkling with joy, while the other animals danced and sang around them.

From that day on, the enchanted forest of the flying foxes was safe once more. The bats and the other animals lived in harmony, protected by the magic of their home and the bond of their friendship. And though the humans may have been gone, the magic of the forest remained, a testament to the power of love and friendship in the face of danger.

Over time, the flying foxes became the guardians of the enchanted forest, ensuring that it remained safe from harm. They continued to play their games and sing their songs, but now they did so with a sense of responsibility and pride.

One day, a young rabbit named Reginald stumbled upon the enchanted forest. He had been wandering through the woods, searching for adventure, when he heard the sweet melodies of the flying foxes and followed the sound.

As he stepped into the clearing, he was awed by the beauty of the place. The trees were tall and lush, the flowers shimmered in the sunlight, and the air was filled with the scent of magic.

Reginald soon discovered that the forest was home to many magical creatures, including the flying foxes, who welcomed him with open wings. They taught him how to play their games and sing their songs, and Reginald quickly fell in love with the enchanted world.

But soon, he learned of the danger that the forest had faced and how the flying foxes had worked together with the other animals to protect it. He knew then that he too had a duty to help keep the forest safe.

And so, Sir Reginald Rabbit became the newest member of the enchanted forest's guardians. With his quick wit and boundless energy, he helped the flying foxes and the other animals to keep watch over the forest, and together, they ensured that it remained a place of wonder and magic for all who entered.

Years passed, and Sir Reginald Rabbit grew old and wise. He watched as generations of flying foxes and other animals came and went, but the magic of the enchanted forest remained strong.

And though he knew that he would one day pass on to the next adventure, he also knew that the magic of the forest would live on, carried forward by the love and friendship of all who called it home.

43

The Great Escape of the Red-Eyed Tree Frog

---◦◇◦---

Once upon a time, in a dense jungle in South America, there lived a red-eyed tree frog named Freddy. Freddy was a curious and adventurous frog who loved exploring the jungle and meeting new creatures. One day, while hopping from tree to tree, he stumbled upon a group of mischievous monkeys who were planning their escape from the zoo.

Freddy was intrigued by the monkeys' plan and decided to join in on the fun. The monkeys had already figured out how to get past the guards, but they needed a distraction to create a diversion. Freddy, being the quick-thinking frog that he was, offered to create the distraction by drawing the guards' attention away from the monkeys.

The night of the escape arrived, and Freddy was nervous but excited. He climbed up a nearby tree and began croaking loudly. The guards, startled by the noise, shone their flashlights in Freddy's direction. Freddy quickly hopped to another tree, and the guards followed him, trying to catch him.

As they chased him through the jungle, Freddy led them on a wild goose chase, jumping from tree to tree and making loud croaking sounds. Meanwhile, the monkeys made their escape, and soon they were all safely out of the zoo.

After the great escape, Freddy returned to his usual routine of exploring the jungle. However, he was now a hero among the animals for his bravery and quick thinking. They all looked up to him and admired his adventurous spirit.

From that day on, whenever there was a problem in the jungle, the animals knew they could count on Freddy to come up with a creative solution. And Freddy lived happily ever after, knowing that he had made a difference in the lives of his fellow creatures.

One day, while on one of his jungle explorations, Freddy stumbled upon a group of baby tree frogs who were lost and alone. Freddy knew that he had to help them find their way back to their families, so he offered to guide them through the jungle.

As they journeyed through the dense foliage, Freddy told the baby tree frogs stories of his many adventures and the lessons he had learned along the way. He showed them how to find food and water and how to stay safe from predators. The baby tree frogs looked up to Freddy with admiration, and he felt a sense of fulfillment knowing that he was able to help them.

After several hours of traveling, they finally found the baby tree frogs' families. Freddy was greeted with warm thanks and gratitude, and he felt a sense of belonging among the tree frog community. From then on, the baby tree frogs became Freddy's loyal followers and joined him on his many adventures through the jungle.

As the years went by, Freddy continued to lead the way for the animals of the jungle, always ready to lend a helping hand and share his wisdom. He became known as the great adventurer and protector of the jungle, and his legend lived on even after he was gone.

To this day, the animals of the jungle tell stories of the great escape of the red-eyed tree frog and the many adventures of Freddy, the bravest and most adventurous frog of them all.

44

The Legend of the Diamond Dragon

—•◦◇◦•—

Long ago, in a kingdom far, far away, there was a powerful and mysterious creature known as the Diamond Dragon. This dragon was said to be made entirely of diamonds, with shimmering scales that sparkled in the sunlight. It was said that anyone who could capture the Diamond Dragon would become the wealthiest and most powerful person in all the land.

Many brave warriors and adventurers set out to find the Diamond Dragon, but none returned. The dragon was said to be protected by powerful magic and deadly traps, and many believed it was impossible to capture.

However, one day, a young orphan boy named Jack decided to set out on his own quest to find the Diamond Dragon. Jack had nothing to his name, but he was determined to find the dragon and claim its treasure. He traveled through treacherous mountains and across vast deserts, facing many dangers along the way.

Finally, after many months of traveling, Jack arrived at the entrance to the Diamond Dragon's lair. He took a deep breath, summoned all his courage, and stepped inside. The lair was dark and filled with traps, but Jack was quick-witted and managed to avoid them all.

As he got deeper into the lair, he saw the shimmering scales of the Diamond Dragon. The dragon was sleeping, so Jack approached it slowly, being careful not to wake it. He reached out and touched the dragon, and to his amazement, the dragon did not stir.

Jack quickly realized that the Diamond Dragon was not alive. It was a statue made entirely of diamonds, but it was so lifelike that it fooled even the bravest of adventurers. Jack smiled to himself, knowing that he had outsmarted all those who had come before him.

He grabbed the statue and ran out of the lair as quickly as he could. He knew that the Diamond Dragon's treasure was his, and he would be the richest person in all the land. As he emerged from the lair, he was greeted by cheers and applause from the villagers who had been watching from a distance.

From that day on, Jack was known as the hero who captured the Diamond Dragon. He used his newfound wealth to help the poor and needy, and he lived the rest of his life in luxury and happiness. And although the legend of the Diamond Dragon lived on, Jack knew the truth about the statue, and he was content with the knowledge that he had outsmarted the dragon and all those who had tried to capture it before him.

As the years went by, the legend of the Diamond Dragon continued to grow, and people from all over the world came to see the statue that had fooled so many brave adventurers. They marveled at its beauty and the incredible story of how a young orphan boy had managed to capture it.

As for Jack, he became a wise and respected leader in his community. He used his wealth and influence to build schools and hospitals, and to help those in need. He never forgot the lessons he had learned on his quest for the Diamond Dragon, and he remained humble and kind to everyone he met.

Years later, when Jack was an old man, he returned to the Diamond Dragon's lair one last time. He sat beside the statue, and he thought about all the adventures he had been on and all the people he had helped. He realized that the true treasure he had found was not the diamonds but the memories and the lessons he had learned along the way.

Jack smiled to himself and closed his eyes, knowing that his life had been a great adventure, and that he had made a difference in the world. And as the sun set over the mountains, he whispered to himself, "Thank you, Diamond Dragon, for showing me that true wealth is not found in treasure, but in the journey itself."

45

The Secret Life of the Underwater World

·◦◇◦·

Deep beneath the surface of the ocean lies a secret world, filled with strange and wondrous creatures that few humans have ever seen. This is the world of the underwater creatures, where schools of colorful fish swim through coral reefs, and giant whales roam the open seas.

But there is more to this world than meets the eye. Beneath the waves, there are hidden caves and grottos, where creatures live in complete darkness. There are also vast underwater plains, where creatures glide effortlessly through the water, and deep trenches where the pressure is so intense that only the most resilient creatures can survive.

One of the most incredible creatures in this underwater world is the giant squid. These massive creatures can grow up to 43 feet long and weigh up to 600 pounds. They live in the deepest parts of the ocean, where the water is so dark that few creatures can survive.

The giant squid has long been a mystery to humans, and for many years, scientists believed that they were nothing more than a myth. But thanks to modern technology and deep-sea exploration, we now know that these creatures are very real.

Another fascinating creature of the underwater world is the bioluminescent jellyfish. These jellyfish are able to produce their own light, creating a beautiful and otherworldly glow in the darkness of the ocean. They are found in all parts of the ocean, from shallow coral reefs to the darkest depths of the abyss.

But the underwater world is not just about creatures. There are also incredible geological formations, such as underwater mountains and volcanic vents. These vents are home to a diverse ecosystem of creatures that thrive in the extreme conditions.

As we continue to explore and learn about the underwater world, we uncover new secrets and mysteries. And as we do, we come to appreciate the incredible diversity and beauty of the creatures that live in this hidden world, reminding us that there is still so much we have yet to discover about our planet.

46

The Misadventures of a Talking Parrot

---•◇•---

Percy was a talking parrot who had a bit of an attitude problem. He lived in a pet store and loved nothing more than to squawk loudly and insult the customers who came in to look at him.

One day, a young couple came into the store and fell in love with Percy's colorful feathers and chatty personality. They decided to adopt him and take him home.

But once they got him home, they quickly realized that Percy was not the friendly, talkative bird they had hoped for. He refused to talk to them, and when he did, it was usually to insult them or make rude comments.

One day, the couple had enough of Percy's bad attitude and decided to take him to a bird trainer. The trainer worked with Percy, teaching him how to speak politely and behave himself.

But Percy was not interested in being polite. He escaped from the trainer's facility and flew off into the city.

As he soared through the sky, Percy began to realize that his attitude was getting him nowhere. He started to feel lonely and longed for the companionship of his owners.

So Percy decided to return to his owners' home, but he didn't know how to find his way back. He flew around the city, searching for any sign of familiarity.

After several hours of searching, Percy finally spotted his owners' apartment building. He landed on the balcony and knocked on the glass door with his beak.

When his owners saw him, they were overjoyed. They welcomed him back with open arms and promised to be more patient with him.

Percy had learned his lesson and realized that sometimes it's better to be kind and polite rather than rude and insulting. From then on, he made an effort to be a better bird, and his owners were grateful to have him back as a loving and talkative companion.

As Percy settled back into his life with his owners, he began to enjoy his newfound manners. He found that he got more attention and treats from his owners when he spoke politely and behaved well. He even started to make friends with the other birds in the neighborhood, who appreciated his improved attitude.

One day, while he was chatting with his new bird friends, Percy overheard a group of pigeons talking about a local bird talent show. The winner would receive a lifetime supply of birdseed, and Percy couldn't resist the temptation to enter.

With the help of his owners, Percy practiced his singing and dancing routines every day leading up to the talent show. He even came up with a few new jokes that were both funny and polite.

On the day of the talent show, Percy was nervous but excited. He performed his routines flawlessly, impressing the judges and the audience with his newfound manners and charm.

And when the winner was announced, Percy was overjoyed to hear his name called out. He had won the lifetime supply of birdseed, and he knew that his owners would be proud of him.

From that day on, Percy continued to work on his manners and kindness. He discovered that being polite and friendly was not only good for him, but it also made the world a better place. And he knew that he would never go back to his old, rude ways again.

47

The Mysterious Island of the Siren Song

———•◦◇◦•———

Legend has it that there is an island in the middle of the ocean, where a beautiful and haunting song can be heard for miles around. Sailors who hear the song are said to be lured to the island by the Siren's enchanting voice, never to be seen again.

Many sailors have tried to find this mysterious island, but few have returned to tell the tale. However, one group of adventurous explorers, led by a fearless captain named Elena, were determined to find the island and solve its mysteries once and for all.

As they sailed across the vast ocean, the sound of the Siren's song grew louder and more alluring. But Elena and her crew had come prepared. They wore earplugs and carried special equipment designed to detect the source of the Siren's song.

After weeks of sailing, they finally spotted the island in the distance. It was shrouded in mist and surrounded by treacherous rocks and cliffs.

As they approached the island, the Siren's song grew even louder, and Elena's crew started to feel its powerful pull. But they held fast and continued on, determined to find out the truth about the island and its mysterious song.

They navigated their way through the treacherous rocks and found a hidden cove where they could anchor their ship. As they stepped ashore, they felt the island's strange power over them. The air was thick with mist, and the sound of the Siren's song was deafening.

Elena and her crew searched the island, looking for the source of the song. They found a cave deep in the heart of the island, where a beautiful woman with a voice like an angel was singing the haunting melody.

But Elena was not fooled. She knew that the woman was not a Siren but a talented singer who had been stranded on the island for years. The woman had been using her voice to lure sailors to the island in hopes of being rescued.

Elena and her crew helped the woman off the island and returned her to civilization. And with her gone, the island's spell was broken. The Siren's song faded away, and the island became just another dot on the map.

But Elena and her crew would never forget the power of the mysterious island and the lure of the Siren's song. And they knew that they had uncovered a mystery that would continue to captivate and intrigue sailors for years to come.

As Elena and her crew set sail from the island, they were filled with a sense of accomplishment and adventure. They knew that they had solved the mystery of the Siren's song, but they also knew that there were many more mysteries waiting to be uncovered in the vast ocean.

As they sailed back towards civilization, they encountered storms and sea monsters, but they faced each challenge head-on with courage and determination. Elena became known as a fearless captain, and her crew was respected throughout the land for their bravery and skill.

Years later, Elena retired from sailing and settled down in a small coastal town. She would often sit by the shore, listening to the sound of the waves and remembering the adventures of her youth.

But every once in a while, she would hear a haunting melody on the wind, and she would smile to herself, knowing that the mysteries of the ocean were still waiting to be discovered. And perhaps one day, she would set sail once again, to explore the unknown and unravel the secrets of the sea.

48

The Incredible Journey of the Caterpillar

---◦◇◦---

Once upon a time, in a lush garden filled with colorful flowers and trees, a tiny caterpillar was born. As she crawled along the ground, she marveled at the beauty of the world around her and dreamed of one day exploring it all.

As the days passed, the caterpillar grew bigger and stronger, eating her way through the garden and transforming herself into a beautiful butterfly. But her journey was only beginning.

One day, as the butterfly was flying over the garden, she caught a glimpse of a distant mountain range. She knew that she had to see them up close and feel the wind in her wings as she soared over their peaks.

Without a second thought, the butterfly set off on her incredible journey, flying over rivers, valleys, and forests, dodging predators and facing countless challenges along the way.

As she flew higher and higher towards the mountains, she felt a sense of freedom and wonder that she had never felt before. She knew that anything was possible if she believed in herself and followed her dreams.

Finally, after many days of flying, the butterfly reached the foot of the mountains. She landed on a flower and gazed up at the towering peaks, knowing that she had accomplished something truly incredible.

But the butterfly's journey was not yet over. She knew that there were many more adventures waiting for her, and she was determined to explore them all. So she spread her wings and took off once again, soaring towards the horizon and the endless possibilities that lay ahead.

And so, the incredible journey of the caterpillar turned butterfly continued, filled with wonder, adventure, and the knowledge that anything was possible if one dared to dream and never gave up on their journey.

As the butterfly flew over the mountains, she noticed a group of birds perched on a tree. They seemed to be in distress and the butterfly decided to investigate.

She landed on a nearby branch and listened as the birds explained that their nest had been destroyed in a storm, leaving their young chicks without shelter. They were desperate for a new home and didn't know where to turn.

The butterfly knew that she could help. She fluttered her wings and summoned her animal friends from all around. Together, they set out to find a new home for the birds and their chicks.

They searched high and low, exploring every corner of the mountain range until finally, they found a perfect spot for the birds to build their new nest. It was a cozy spot under the shade of a tall tree, with plenty of branches and twigs for the birds to use.

The butterfly and her friends worked tirelessly to help the birds build their new home, and before long, the nest was complete. The birds were overjoyed and thanked the butterfly for her help.

Feeling a sense of satisfaction from having helped her animal friends, the butterfly took to the skies once again, ready for whatever adventures lay ahead. She knew that wherever she went, she would always find a way to help those in need and continue on her incredible journey.

And so, the journey of the caterpillar turned butterfly continued, filled with adventure, wonder, and the knowledge that even the smallest creature can make a big difference in the world.

49

The Amazing Adventures of the Pocket-Sized Hero

———•◦◇◦•———

In a far-off land, where magic and wonder were commonplace, there lived a small and unassuming hero. He was no bigger than a thumb, but his heart was full of bravery and determination.

The hero lived in a small village in the middle of a dense forest, where he spent his days exploring the world around him and helping those in need. Despite his size, he had a quick mind and was always ready for adventure.

One day, while exploring the forest, the hero stumbled upon a group of travelers who had been ambushed by bandits. They were in desperate need of help and the hero knew that he had to act fast.

Using his wit and quick reflexes, the hero was able to outsmart the bandits and save the travelers from harm. They were grateful for his help and invited him to join them on their journey.

Together, they traveled to distant lands and encountered all manner of danger and excitement. They battled dragons, rescued princesses, and even saved a kingdom from a wicked sorcerer.

Despite the dangers they faced, the hero never lost his courage and determination. He always found a way to overcome the obstacles in his path and help those in need.

As the years passed, the hero became known throughout the land as a pocket-sized champion of justice and bravery. People would come from far and wide to seek his help and he was always ready to lend a hand.

But despite his fame and success, the hero never lost his humble nature. He continued to explore the world around him, always seeking new adventures and challenges.

And so, the amazing adventures of the pocket-sized hero continued, filled with wonder, excitement, and the knowledge that even the smallest person can make a big difference in the world.

One day, the hero received a call for help from a far-off land that he had never visited before. The people of this land were facing a terrible threat from a giant monster that was terrorizing their village.

The hero knew that he had to help, so he set out on a long journey across mountains, deserts, and oceans. When he arrived at the village, he saw the destruction that the monster had caused and knew that this would be his toughest challenge yet.

Undaunted, the hero set about finding a way to defeat the monster. He explored the village and talked to the people, learning everything he could about the monster and its weaknesses.

Finally, he came up with a plan. He would use his small size and agility to outsmart the monster and strike at its weak spots. With the help of the villagers, he set his plan into action.

For hours, the hero battled the monster, darting in and out of its grasp, dodging its attacks, and striking at its weak points. The monster was strong, but the hero was quicker and more cunning.

In the end, the hero emerged victorious. The monster lay defeated, and the village was saved. The people cheered and celebrated, grateful for the hero's bravery and skill.

With his mission accomplished, the hero bid farewell to the people of the village and set out once again on his never-ending journey. He knew that there would always be more adventures and challenges to face, and he was eager to see what lay ahead.

And so, the amazing adventures of the pocket-sized hero continued, filled with excitement, wonder, and the knowledge that even the smallest hero can make a big difference in the world.

50

The Secret Society of the Time-Travelers

$\bullet\!\!\circ\!\!\diamond\!\!\circ\!\!\bullet$

In a world beyond our own, there existed a secret society of time-travelers. They were a group of elite individuals who had mastered the art of time-travel and used their abilities to preserve the flow of history and prevent catastrophic events from happening.

The society was shrouded in secrecy, and only a select few knew of its existence. The time-travelers operated in secret, working tirelessly to ensure that the timeline remained intact.

One day, a young woman named Samantha stumbled upon the society by accident. She had always been fascinated by history and had spent countless hours studying the past. Little did she know, her knowledge had caught the attention of the time-travelers.

Impressed by her intelligence and passion for history, the society invited Samantha to join them. She was hesitant at first, but the thought of being able to travel through time was too tempting to resist.

Samantha was trained rigorously by the society's most experienced time-travelers. She learned the ins and outs of time-travel, the dangers of altering history, and the importance of maintaining the timeline.

As she embarked on her first mission, Samantha was filled with excitement and nervousness. She traveled back to ancient Greece, where she was tasked with preventing a catastrophic event that would have altered the course of history.

Using her knowledge of the past and the skills she had learned from the time-travelers, Samantha succeeded in her mission. The timeline was preserved, and history continued to unfold as it was meant to.

Over time, Samantha became one of the society's most accomplished time-travelers. She traveled to different eras and countries, preventing disasters, and preserving the timeline. But despite her success, she never forgot the importance of her mission or the responsibility that came with it.

As Samantha continued on her adventures through time, she marveled at the wonders of history and the incredible journey that lay ahead of her. The secret society of time-travelers continued to work in the shadows, preserving the flow of history and keeping the world safe from harm.

However, Samantha soon realized that the society was not as perfect as she had believed. There were those who used their abilities for their own gain, altering history to suit their own desires. Samantha found herself in a dilemma - should she expose these rogue time-travelers and risk breaking the society's code of secrecy?

As she struggled with her decision, Samantha discovered that there was an even greater threat to the timeline. A powerful force was attempting to alter history on a massive scale, threatening to plunge the world into chaos.

Samantha knew that she could not face this threat alone. She gathered a team of the society's most trusted time-travelers, and together they set out to stop the looming disaster.

Their journey took them to different eras and countries, as they battled against the powerful force trying to alter history. With each victory, they grew stronger and more determined to preserve the timeline and protect the world from harm.

In the end, Samantha and her team emerged victorious. They had saved the timeline from a catastrophic alteration and ensured that history continued to unfold as it was meant to.

As the secret society of time-travelers continued their work in the shadows, Samantha realized that the responsibility of preserving history was not just theirs alone. It was a responsibility that rested on the shoulders of everyone, and it was up to each individual to do their part in shaping the course of history.

And so, Samantha continued on her adventures through time, knowing that the future was in her hands and that the past was just as important as the present. The secret society of time-travelers remained shrouded in secrecy, working tirelessly to ensure that history remained unchanged and that the world was safe from harm.

Top of Form

Top of Form

Book description

Whimsical Wonders: 50 Tales of Fictional Fun is a delightful collection of stories that will capture your imagination and transport you to a world of whimsy and wonder. These stories are a product of the creative mind of Mr. Derick Chibilu, a lover of fun and fanciful tales.

Whether you're a child or an adult, you'll find something to love in this collection. The stories are crafted to be engaging, entertaining, and imaginative, providing a much-needed escape from the stresses of everyday life.

Mr. Chibilu has poured his heart and soul into creating these tales, and it shows in the quality of the writing. Each story is unique and original, with colorful characters, surprising plot twists, and a healthy dose of humor. From talking animals to enchanted forests, from brave heroes to mischievous fairies, these stories will captivate your imagination and leave you wanting more.

This collection is perfect for reading on the go - whether you're on a long flight, waiting at the doctor's office, or taking a break from the hustle and bustle of daily life. The stories are also ideal for bedtime reading, as they are suitable for all ages and will inspire sweet dreams and playful imaginations.

If you're looking for a collection of fun and lighthearted stories that will make you smile, Whimsical Wonders: 50 Tales of Fictional Fun is the book for you. So why not pick up a copy today and join Mr. Chibilu on a journey through his imaginative world of whimsy and wonder? You won't be disappointed!

ABOUT THE AUTHOR

————•◦◇◦•————

Derick Chibilu is a proud resident of Houston, Texas where he lives with his beloved wife, Alice. He is an aspiring blogger and business professional, with a passion for writing that has led him to create some of the most inspiring works in recent years. Derick's educational background includes an MBA from Capella University, a Bachelor of Business in Computer Information Systems, and an Associate of Science in Business Administration.

Derick's faith is an integral part of his life, as he is a born-again Christian who is deeply committed to his beliefs. He is an active member of the North Central Assemblies of God Church in Spring Texas, where he finds inspiration and strength in fellowship with other believers. Derick strongly believes in God, family, and Christian family values, which are themes that are central to his writing.

As an author, Derick has a unique talent for bringing complex topics to life in a way that is both accessible and engaging. He has written extensively on a range of subjects, including business, leadership, personal development, and Christian spirituality. His works have been praised for their clarity, insight, and practicality, making them a valuable resource for readers from all walks of life.

In addition to his non-fiction works, Derick recently published his first fiction book, Whimsical Wonders: 50 Tales of Fictional Fun. This collection of short stories showcases Derick's creativity and imagination and has been well-received by readers of all ages. The book is a departure from his usual genre but showcases his versatility as a writer.

Derick's commitment to excellence is evident in everything he does. He is a dedicated professional who takes pride in his work, and he is always seeking new ways to improve himself and his craft. Whether he is writing a new book, giving a speech, or leading a team, Derick brings the same level of passion and enthusiasm to everything he does.

In short, Derick Chibilu is an inspiring author and business professional who is making a difference in the world. His faith, his family, and his commitment to Christian values have shaped his life and his work, and his writing has the power to inspire and uplift readers around the globe.

CPSIA information can be obtained
at www.ICGtesting.com
Printed in the USA
BVHW030527120423
662150BV00006B/285

9 781088 076965